Last Scene at Balthazar's Theatre

Lee Koss

Copyright © 2022 Lee Koss.

All rights reserved. No part of this publication may be reproduced, distributed, or transmitted in any form or by any means, including photocopying, recording, or other electronic or mechanical methods, without the prior written permission of the author, except in the case of brief quotations embodied in critical reviews and certain other noncommercial uses permitted by copyright law.

ISBN: 9798830907132

Any references to historical events, real people, or real places are used fictitiously. Names, characters, and places are products of the author's imagination.

Front cover image by Clensos

First printing edition 2022

Email : leekossbooks@gmail.com

Website : aqua-marlin-d62r.squarespace.com

About the author

Lee Koss, *nom de plume*, lives in the Vaud Canton, Switzerland. Prior to his writing career, he worked in marketing and communications.

Last Scene at Balthazar's Theatre is the author's second published novel, following *Murkier than the Mersey*, set in Liverpool, England.

This is a work of fiction. Unless otherwise indicated, all the names, characters, businesses, places, events, and incidents in this book are either the product of the author's imagination or used in a fictitious manner.

Any resemblance to actual persons, living or dead, or actual events is purely coincidental.

Jorat Region, Vaud Canton, Switzerland

PART ONE

Mid-to-end December

Chapter One

Wednesday late morning, December 22, Mézières, Vaud Canton, Switzerland

Marianne Devaud parked her ten-year-old Peugeot 206 just down the road from her Mum's third-floor flat in Mézières, a small village twenty minutes' drive from the city of Lausanne, capital of the Canton of Vaud in the French-speaking part of Switzerland.

Her African, Gambian mother lived in a low-cost apartment next to the village bakery. Entering without knocking, she called out to her mother in English, 'Hi Mum, it's me. Is Dani here? Oh, and have you seen my phone? Think I left it here yesterday.'

The three-bedroom apartment was warm and cosily appointed. Oriental rugs covered the tiled floors. On the shelves in the sitting room stood a series of elegant and beautifully carved wooden sculptures of African women, some with babies in their arms. A tasteful picture of the silver crescent moon, on a deep blue background, hung in the hallway. The walls were painted in vibrant colours, and lush green tropical plants lined the corridors and the windowsills. The heating was regulated to twenty-five degrees Celsius. It was warm, almost tropical inside the Devaud home.

This had been Marianne's only home until she'd finished her bachelor's degree in criminology at the University of Lausanne two years earlier. She was now in the middle of her doctorate in the same field and rented a room in the city, though recently she'd been staying more at her boyfriend's place in a nearby village called Montpreveyres. She'd driven here from his place this morning.

Marianne had not yet decided whether she wanted to be a police officer or whether she was better fitted to become a criminal psychologist. No hurry. She still had time to decide, with another year remaining before finishing her thesis. She was now on a six-month internship with the police, which would help her decide.

Marianne's natural beauty was disguised in her tomboy attitude. She hardly ever noticed the lustful looks she received from the men around her until her friends began to point them out. She'd remained somewhat naïve about her good natural looks.

Outside the home, she always kept her hair in an Afro-bun, wore jeans and a baggy jersey most of the time, and never stepped out without her black Doc Martens boots. Marianne never felt the need to wear high heels to appear taller. What for? She was happy. And she was feisty.

This morning she was looking for her brother, Dani Devaud, a professional football player who was now paid for his talents in the English Football League Championship for Wigan Athletic FC.

'No, my sweet. I thought he stayed with you at your new man's flat last night. What's his name again?'

'It doesn't matter Mum. Dani wasn't with us, and I wanted to catch up with him before he flies back to England.'

'Well, my dear, so would I, after all that business last night. Didn't' you hear?'

'No, what happened?'

'At the theatre. You know. The anniversary fund-raiser for Jorat Mézières Football Club. Françoise downstairs told me there was some sort of power outage and the fire alarm kicked off. Police, fire trucks, ambulances, the works. Old Balthazar had to cancel the event at the end of the first half and send everyone home. That's why I thought Dani must've gone to stay with you and your latest man, what's his name again?'

'Kenosha, Mum, but that doesn't matter. I just want to know where Dani is.'

'That doesn't sound a very Swiss name, Kenosha? Don't tell me he's African, like your good old momma? Because if he is, beware, my girl, beware! Can't trust African men, especially those Gambians, ha, ha,' she laughed, only half-joking.

Marianne Devaud was always very careful when she talked *men* with her mother. She was about to turn twenty-six and had still never plucked up the courage to bring a boyfriend home to meet her Mum. Her father, a local Swiss white man, had met her mother on vacation in The Gambia in the early 1990s. They'd been a very loving and passionate couple until drink got the better of him. He now lived rough in neighbouring France with his dog.

Not surprisingly, Marianne's mother was constantly warning her to stay away from men who drank, even the smallest drop. Then again, she didn't want Marianne to hook up with a teetotal Muslim, saying she didn't trust them either. They could be terrorists. She didn't like any foreigner much, even though she was one herself. What she wanted for her girl was a nice young Swiss man with a steady job. Maybe a policeman? Her new man Kenosha was a policeman, but Marianne preferred to wait a while before having him meet her mother, whose attitude reminded her of that old Swiss saying - *plus Suisse que les Suisses* – more Swiss than the Swiss. This is what many foreigners became when they took Swiss nationality.

Marianne's experience had been different. Growing up in their small Swiss village of Mézières, both she and her brother Dani had received occasional *remarks* related to their skin pigmentation, mostly in supposed *jest*. They'd quickly learned to shrug them off and were both sufficiently gritty not to let it get them down. In any case, as their mother never stopped reminding them, they had five hundred years of Mézières village, Vaud Canton, Swiss lineage running through their veins thanks to their forever absent, hobo Dad, whose name was no longer ever mentioned in the otherwise happy Devaud household.

There were plenty of foreign kids in the village. Kosovars, Serbians, Italians, Portuguese, Spanish, Scots, Germans, and others. But they were white and had never had to pretend to ignore some older members calling them *les blacks du village*.

'You know what Dani's like. Marianne. He'll turn up. He always does. Never one to tell his old Mum where he was going.'

Marianne was not convinced. 'I'll go check in his bedroom. Maybe he sneaked in while you were asleep, or talking with Françoise downstairs? Got to find my phone as well. I may have left it here.'

As Marianne disappeared down the corridor to Dani's old bedroom, her mum glanced affectionately at the large, framed photo on the table in the entryway: Dani Devaud, Granit Berisha, and Marco Zurcher, all smiling in their FC Jorat Mézières football kit. Twelve or thirteen years old were they when that picture was taken? She picked up the frame and stared lovingly at the kids. Those three. The *Brio Trio*. Inseparable from their early childhood. Then something must have happened when they'd hit eighteen when Granit suddenly became much more distant. Probably because he was famous, she thought. Whatever. Granit's a good lad all the same, even if he's got more distant these days, she thought.

The *Brio Trio* had all started their football together aged six at the local club, FCJM, the abbreviation for Jorat-Mézières football club. By the time they'd reached their teens, all three had been recruited to the Lausanne Sports Football Club Academy. And they'd all played for the Swiss national teams from the under fifteen to the under nineteen. It was then that Granit was scooped up by Liverpool FC of the English Premier League, the richest national league in the world.

Now worth tens of millions, Granit Berisha was at the pinnacle of his career. Aged twenty-eight, he led the attack for the Reds at Anfield and was fast becoming their all-time best goal scorer. He'd already been nominated twice for the UEFA Men's Player of the Year Award, though he'd not yet won that top accolade, losing out to the likes of Cristiano Ronaldo, Lionel Messi, and fellow Liverpool teammate Virgil van Dijk. Not bad company.

Granit's luxurious life as a professional footballer in England today was such a long way from his poor childhood, where his father had washed dishes in the kitchen of a local theatre and his mother had been a domestic cleaner, without valid work permits for the first years. His parents, who'd escaped the war in ex-Yugoslavia in the 1990s, had now returned to their native Kosovo where they lived like royalty on the money Granit, their one and only child, sent them every month.

Brio Trio number two, Marco Zurcher had stuck with Lausanne Sports FC and remained a pillar of the team's midfield. For his part, *Brio Trio* number three, Dani Devaud, a quick and sprightly midfielder, had already changed teams twice in the English leagues, moving down the pecking order from Everton FC to Wigan Athletic FC. These were teams located in the northwest of England, a region that had become Dani's adopted home. Dani now lived less than thirty kilometers from Granit, but they never saw each other off the football field these days.

The success of the *Brio Trio* on the football field and the personal wealth that it had generated for all three, most of all for Granit, was due in large part to two influential people in their youth: Ray *Weymo* McCauley, and football agent Dirk de Clippele.

Coach McCauley had moved from Dumbarton in west Scotland to Switzerland to teach English at the Lausanne Hotel School in the 1980s. When Ray's son started playing football for Mézières junior team at the age of seven, he'd volunteered to train the kid's team in his spare time.

He'd never looked back, becoming President of the club in the early noughties.

Ray's nickname *Weymo* came from the younger kids, unable to pronounce the letter *R* of Raymond's full name. The name stuck, and everyone at the club now called him Weymo.

Coach Weymo met Dirk de Clippele when the under-twelve team he was coaching won the regional cup competition, beating the bigger and wealthier Geneva Servette and Lausanne Sports FC under-twelve teams along the way.

Dirk de Clippele, now in his late fifties like Coach Weymo, had always wanted to play at the international level for his native Belgium. And he'd been blessed with the talent and skills to get there. But after a couple of serious injuries as a teenager, his father pulled him off the football pitch and into the abattoir he owned, where Dirk worked as a butcher until his mid-twenties.

During his time at the abattoir, Dirk remained passionate about football, visiting small clubs each weekend to discover talented young players. Little by little he'd gained a reputation as a football scout, discovering a host of high-potential players across Belgium.

Over the next few years, he built a strong network of scouts around the European continent and had now become one of the highest-paid football agents in Europe. It helped that he spoke five languages fluently, though Dirk considered this quite normal for Flemish Belgians.

The top-paying asset on his books today was Swiss international Granit Berisha, by a large margin. Dirk also continued to manage Granit's old mates Dani Devaud and Marco Zurcher, but they were paupers in comparison to the great Granit. Dirk often joked with Anita Patel, his English lawyer, and part-time lover, that he managed Dani and Marco as charity cases, and out of loyalty to Coach Weymo.

Reflecting nostalgically, Marianne's mum put the photo back down on the entryway table. What great kids and what luck they'd had to meet Weymo and Dirk so early in their lives to help guide them on their way into the professional football world. She put her head down and said a thankful prayer of gratitude.

Suddenly she was woken from her contemplation by a panicked scream.

'Mum, mum!'

Marianne was half-walking, half-stumbling, confusedly, back down the corridor from Dani's old bedroom, mobile phone in hand.

'This can't be true. Please, God. No.'

'What is it, my love? Calm down.'

'Listen, Mum. Listen to the voicemail message from Dani. 9.34 yesterday evening. He can't be dead, surely. If he is, it will be my fault. Oh my God.'

Mrs. Devaud played Dani's message out loud for the two of them to hear on the phone's speaker. The message was difficult to decipher.

Help Marianne. No joke. Think…drugged….drinks. Can't….the. ….scared. Freezing in here. Don't …die. Help. Quick…..now…..soon.

Chapter Two

The previous day, Tuesday, December 21, Balthazar's Theatre, Servion, Vaud Canton

Townsfolk from Lausanne, Montreux, Vevey, and other cities and towns in the Vaud canton called the *Jorat* region the *land of the wolves*. But the only wolves remaining, were those confined to a corner of the zoo in Servion, the next-door village to Mézières. They were there with the bears, tigers, lions, boars, bison, and a whole range of other animals that attracted thousands of visitors to the small village of Servion each year. It was a well-managed zoo, which prided itself on numerous births each year as well as a top reputation among other zoos in Europe.

In addition to the zoo, Servion boasted its own famous theatre, *Balthazar's*. A large and imposing wooden structure on the road from Vevey to Moudon, the theatre was founded by Monsieur Balthazar Bonzon himself, a born and bred Servion villager. His real name was Thierry, but everyone knew him as Balthazar. The theatre welcomed around twenty-five thousand punters per year. No self-respecting Vaudois would miss the *Annual Revue* where the eccentric Balthazar would hog the stage, mocking the local politicians and celebrities. If you were not featured in Balthazar's annual revue, then you'd not yet made it as a celebrity in Vaud canton.

Balthazar was now in his eighties and had once told a friend he'd rather die on stage than end up in an old people's home. And if the death scene were filmed, all the better. He'd become even more famous dead than alive.

In addition to the theatre and the zoo, there was a third tourist attraction nearby, less well-known: a five-thousand-year-old menhir, the biggest in Switzerland, tucked away at the bottom of a nearby hillside. It stood less than a mile away from the theatre, past the local cemetery and the sewage works on the other side of the small *Parimbot* brook.

Standing at over five metres in height the menhir went by the name of *Pierre du dos de l'âne*. The residents of Servion were also known by the nickname *les ânes* - the Donkeys. Because of that, many had developed a special affection for this ancient mystery from five thousand years ago, even though it was not officially located in their village.

A few of the older village families maintained they were directly descended from the menhir worshippers from that bygone age, though without any DNA connection this was difficult to prove. Maybe one day they'd dig up some old bones and prove their case to the world?

At the theatre that December evening, old Balthazar was briefing his team for tonight's special fund-raising event for the local football team, FC Jorat Mézières. Coach Weymo and Dirk de Clippele were with him, as was Dirk's lawyer, Anita Patel. So were the Brio Trio, led by Granit Berisha, who was now one of the highest-paid footballers in the world.

It was now 6 p.m. and Balthazar was managing the proceedings, seated on his director's highchair on the stage. The others were on lower chairs. There was a table in the middle with the stage instructions for the evening printed out. The stage crew needed to be aligned and working off the same script. Since his three-month stint working as a volunteer in London's West End in the 1970s, Balthazar had systematically added a slogan in English at the bottom of his printed stage instructions: BREAK A LEG.

Balthazar's breathing had deteriorated badly since he'd contracted Covid the previous year. And his heart condition was not getting any better. His doctor had advised him to slow down, but that was impossible for a man with such natural drive and energy.

Balthazar summarised the evening's proceedings and asked Dirk and Weymo to distribute the printed instructions, He needed to remain seated to preserve his legs for his role as Master of Ceremonies. He then dismissed the stage crew with an authoritarian *Break a Leg*!

The stage crew left for their various locations. But Kevin Gillieron remained. 'What's up Kevin?' Balthazar asked, jokingly. Even though Kevin could be Balthazar's grandson, at twenty-eight years old, they were, in fact, second cousins.

'All ok, thanks. Nobody's given me my stage instructions for the show. Can I have them please?'

Before Balthazar could react, Dirk de Clippele jumped up and ran over to Kevin with the printed sheets. 'Thanks, Mr. de Clippele,' replied Kevin, 'and let's *Break a Leg*!'

Kevin returned to his position backstage where he'd manage the curtain and also be responsible for driving a mock ambulance on and off the stage in the last scene before the entr'acte. This was a scene depicting a real event when Weymo broke his leg some years ago on the football pitch before he became President of the club. Dirk de Clippele, the wealthy football agent, had kindly purchased the mock ambulance especially for this fund-raising show.

Kevin sat down at his post next to the curtain, near the central electricity box, and read the stage instructions to himself. *'But why would Uncle B want me to do that?'* Very strange and highly unorthodox, especially for a control freak like Balthazar. Whatever. He's the boss, and he must have his reasons. But why me, he murmured to himself.

Something about this show was going to be different. Very different.

Chapter Three

The same evening, 8.30 p.m.

Granit, Dani, and Marco along with Dirk de Clippele and his company lawyer Anita Patel had eaten supper together in the staff office, away from the spectators, before the show. It was the first time the *Brio Trio* had shared a table since they were teenagers playing for the Swiss under-eighteen team in Spain ten years ago.

At eight-thirty p.m. on the dot, they were escorted into the theatre by a hobbling, determined Balthazar, microphone in hand, to a standing ovation from a generous audience. Most of the punters had a direct connection to the club. Some were committee members and club sponsors; others were ex-players with their families; a few had come from further afield in the hope of meeting Granit Berisha in person or at least getting his autograph, and maybe even winning the evening's amazing lottery, an all-expenses-paid VIP weekend in Liverpool, to see the match between Liverpool and Everton FC.

The audience was seated at tables, both on the ground level and in the balcony areas. They'd been wined and dined and were ready to roll. This was one of the standard hallmarks of Balthazar's theatre: get enough drink down them at the start, and the jokes go down much better.

'Ladies and gentlemen, I give you the magnificent and marvellous Marco Zurcher; the dashing and daring Dani Devaud. And I give you the one and only, the great and glorious Granit Berisha. The soon-to-be GOAT, the greatest of all time at Liverpool FC. Can any three young men make us any prouder to be from our wonderful Jorat region? The land of the wolves, as we call it around here.'

Balthazar then howled like a wolf. This was another of his trademarks, and the audience lapped it up.

'Ladies and gentlemen, you're wondering why our esteemed guests are all dressed up as Santas tonight, with beards and sunglasses? And you're probably also wondering why there are five of them, not three. Sorry, can't tell you now, can I? Be patient and you'll understand better when we run the lottery competition at the entr'acte.'

The audience booed and clapped in parallel oozing both expectation and impatience. Balthazar was enjoying this tremendously. He howled again, wolf-like, as he ended his introductory speech. The very act of holding the microphone and the power it gave him swept his hip and shoulder pains aside, temporarily at least. Better than morphine, he thought, and equally as addictive.

Three months ago, when they were imagining how the fund-raising evening would be structured, Dirk de Clippele had proposed to Coach Weymo and Balthazar that the three footballers, as well as he and Anita, enter the theatre dressed up in Santa costumes to get people into the Christmas spirit.

The winner of the VIP lottery prize would be the person who correctly guessed which player was which in their disguises. They'd need to do this by analyzing the way each player walked onto the stage. Granit was on television most weeks at Liverpool FC, and both Marco and Dani had played a lot for the Swiss national team. So, a of lot people would surely guess correctly.

The names of those who successfully recognized the players would then go into a hat. And Balthazar would draw out the winner. For it to work, each Santa would have a number on the front and back of the Santa outfit. This was to take place at the entr'acte.

Dani was a lot smaller in height than Marco and Granit, so spotting him would be too easy if there were only the three of them disguised as Santas on stage. To counter this, Dirk added two other persons to the group dressed up as Santas: he and Anita. Anita was the same height as Dani, and Dirk the same as both Marco and Granit.

The five of them sat down at their reserved table closest to the stage, back to the audience. Dirk organized their non-alcoholic drinks, with each of them receiving long straws to suck in their fruit juices through their Santa beards, without giving too much of their faces away.

Two minutes later the curtains opened. Let the show begin.

Chapter Four

The same evening, 10.15 p.m., Entr'acte

The first half of the show tracing the history of the club had got the audience in stitches, roaring with laughter, and then had taken them back to a more serious mood in the final scene before the entr'acte. The one where club president and Coach Weymo breaks his leg.

The mock ambulance was now on stage. Fake, of course, but it had still cost Dirk de Clippele a lot of money to have it sprayed and re-coloured in the local bodywork garage just across the road from the theatre. The word had quickly gone around the village that Dirk de Clippele, football agent, was even richer than his famous player clients.

The stage curtains were closed, and Balthazar was there, sitting awkwardly in a highchair addressing the audience directly.

'Ladies and gentlemen. Are you enjoying yourselves?' He waited for the roar, which was more of a faint *aaahhh*.

Once again. 'Ladies and gentlemen, ARE YOU HAVING FUN?' This time the roar came back loud and clear from the audience. 'Who wants to win an all-expenses-paid weekend trip for two to Liverpool, staying in a five-star hotel and watching our great Granit Berisha score a hattrick in the English Premier League?'

Balthazar was playing to the crowd. He was in his element. He wasn't a football fan and would not know who the manager of the Swiss national team was at any moment in time, but he knew how to keep his audience in the palm of his hand.

'Well, Madame, it could be you,' he said pointing to an attractive woman on table six.

'Or it could be you, Monsieur,' to the man on table four.

'Or you, little lad,' looking at an excited thirteen-year-old who was standing up at the back to get a glimpse of the action.'

Balthazar moved onto the subject of the lottery.

'Pay attention now as I'm not going to repeat myself. To win tonight's fantastic lottery prize all you must do is guess which of the five Santas to come on stage are Granit Berisha, Dani Devaud, and Marco Zurcher. All five have numbers on their front and backs. You must match them to the names on the sheets on your tables.'

17

With that, Balthazar asked the five Santas to join him onstage.

'Thank you, gentlemen. You're all looking wonderful tonight. But who's who? Damned if I know. OK, I'll give you a clue. Watch the way they walk.'

Balthazar then asked the Santa with the number one to walk across the stage.

'Recognise that way of walking, ladies, and gentlemen? Dani, Marco, or Granit. Decision time.'

Number one was Granit, who walked across the stage in his typical confident stride and came back into line.

'Number two. Your turn now,' Balthazar said, as Granit took back his place in the line. Number two was Dirk de Clippele, who tried his best to imitate Granit's confident walk, crossing the stage and back, and coming over into line behind Granit.

Balthazar continued. 'Number three, please.'

This was Anita, who walked in as manly a manner as she could across the stage, imitating Dani's gait. She then returned and took her place behind, number two.

'Just two Santas to go, folks. Numbers four and five.'

Balthazar asked number four to cross the stage. He was the smaller of the two remaining Santas. It was Dani. As he started walking toward the other side of the stage, Dani felt his head get dizzy and his mind go cloudy; he felt like puking. He just about made it to the other side of the stage, looking like a drunk – which made the audience laugh - and on his way back collapsed to the ground, centre stage. At this point number five, Marco, attempted to run towards him to help, but he also collapsed just before making it to the middle, where Dani was now lying, groaning, holding his stomach in pain.

Suddenly, BANG! A loud noise, which sounded like a bomb explosion. The lights went out and the theatre was thrown into pitch darkness.

Chapter Five

The same evening, 10.45 p.m.

The theatre remained in total darkness for around three minutes. It seemed much longer. Not knowing whether this was part of the show, most of the audience had remained in place at their tables. Balthazar appeared on the ground floor, just in front of the stage, with a hand torch. He had a microphone in the other hand, but it wasn't working, so he spoke as loudly as he could.

'Ladies and gentlemen. Please excuse this disturbance. No, it's not part of the show and I thank you for being calm and for not panicking. In a couple of minutes, our fire alarm will go off. There is no need to worry. We haven't located a fire, but we've had some issues with the central electricity box and the fire department has been called. Unfortunately, we're going to have to cancel the show now. Our apologies again. Please leave the theatre immediately in an orderly and calm manner. Our stewards will show you the way.'

The atmosphere was calm, but tense at the same time. Nobody panicked. Granit, Dirk, and Anita, who had removed their Santa costumes, sunglasses, and beards, were walking out in line with other audience members. But Dani and Marco were not with them.

It took around fifteen minutes for the theatre to empty. As the audience left, the firefighters arrived and were guided by the stage crew backstage for a thorough inspection. Balthazar had found a chair in the entry foyer and was sitting there apologizing to the audience members as they left, promising free tickets for the next show.

Outside the theatre Dirk was cuddling Anita in his arms. She'd lit up a cigarette and was smoking. *Davidoff Slims* was her brand.

Granit's chauffeur was waiting for him, to take him to Geneva airport for a flight the next morning to Liverpool. For once he was distraught. He needed to talk and for the first time in many years, he decided to sit in the front. Suddenly he felt normal again, in a strange way. Nobody had bugged him as he left the theatre. People appeared more concerned for their safety and security. It seemed nice, for once, not to be the centre of attention.

Before leaving, Granit asked Dirk and Anita if they'd seen Dani and Marco since the lights went out. Dirk assured Grant he'd noticed both Dani and Marco get up and leave through the back of the stage, where they haul the sets in and out from the car park area at the rear of the theatre. No worries, then.

'Amazing how that rush of adrenalin got them up, Granit,' Dirk joked. 'No need to worry mate. They'll be fine. Have a great trip back.'

'Of course,' Granit said. 'That's good news, then?'

'Good news,' replied Dirk. 'As always for us.'

Chapter Six

That same evening, 11.30 p.m.

The theatre was now eerily quiet and empty. Seated around the table were the lead firefighter, a medic from the ambulance that was still parked at the front of the theatre, Balthazar and Fabienne Pasche, the Servion village Mayor, or *Syndique* as the position was called.

It was Fabienne Pasche, in her capacity as *Syndique*, the Mayor of the village, who had insisted that Balthazar hold a debriefing that evening.

Fabienne was a guest of honour at the football club fundraiser. She'd shared a table that evening with close friends Detective Inspector Philippe Favre and his wife Véronique, who was the Pastor at the Protestant church in Mézières.

Fabienne Pasche was born a city girl who had grown up in the centre of Lausanne. She'd studied Communications and Modern Languages at the University of Lausanne. Immediately following her studies, she'd joined *Edipresse*, a media company that owned a host of papers including *24 Heures*, the oldest and biggest selling daily in Vaud Canton. By the time she was thirty-five, she'd risen from intern to editor-in-chief, the youngest since the creation of the journal in 1762.

Following the technological disruption in the 2010s *Edipresse* had been sold to a bigger, Swiss-German media outfit. Fabienne had taken the package and moved on.

Now in her late forties, Fabienne had recently been elected *Syndique* of Servion. The work took more than fifty percent of her time but did not pay very well, so she continued to write articles and produce the odd television documentary as an investigative journalist for the Swiss Television network.

At the table, Balthazar opened the debriefing discussion.

'I don't know what went wrong this evening. And neither do the stage crew, I'm afraid. Shame Kevin Gillieron isn't here to shed more light on what happened from his vantage point at the curtain. Anyhow, there was no fire, and no one was injured, so we can count ourselves lucky.'

Both the firefighter and the medic confirmed Balthazar's analysis and said they'd better be getting off. You never knew where the next emergency was going to happen. Balthazar thanked them vociferously.

'I'm going to have to rush now too,' Balthazar said Fabienne. 'Let's meet again tomorrow afternoon, say 3 p.m. A lot of the actors and most of the stage crew will be there for a rehearsal for our Annual Revue, so they can help us with the analysis, as needed.'

Fabienne Pasche was not happy. 'Don't you think we need to get to the bottom of this now, while it's fresh in our memory? It's not a joke Mr. Bonzon. Somebody seriously sabotaged this evening's event. Lucky no one was hurt.'

'What do you suggest, Madame la Syndique?' Balthazar replied, with the emphasis on *Madame*. Despite spending most of his time in the company of footloose and fancy-free actors and dancers, Balthazar remained an old-fashioned Swiss male chauvinist at heart, a little misogynist even.

'Why not have the police do some digging Monsieur? I can ask Detective Inspector Favre to join us tomorrow at three?' Fabienne Pasche replied.

'I bet you can, *Madame* la Syndique. And what else could you have him do for you?' Balthazar knew very well how to push Fabienne's buttons.

Fabienne ignored the inuendo.

'Look, there's no harm in having a second opinion. I'll get him here tomorrow. Basta. No further discussion.'

With that, Fabienne stood up and left the meeting, without saying goodbye to Balthazar.

Old Balthazar remained in his seat. Favre and our dear Syndique, he pondered. Lovers again?

Chapter Seven

Early hours, Wednesday, December 22, 1 a.m.

With everyone gone, Balthazar closed and locked the theatre doors. He waited outside. The dark rain clouds had cleared, and the full moon was now out. Perfect, he thought. Could not be better. The standing stone – our menhir's shadow - will be deep and powerful. Mother nature is with us, as she always is on this special day.

On the stroke of 1 a.m. Kevin Gillieron pulled up in front of the main door at the wheel of the very same mock ambulance used for the final scene of the first act.

'Where the hell have you been Kevin? That Fabienne Pasche Syndique woman has been snooping.'

'Sorry, Uncle B. Was tied up with other stuff.'

'OK, Kevin. Tell me later. Now let's get going before it's light. Shame we'll have to drive there for this winter's homage. Much better walking, as we usually do, but my legs wouldn't make it.'

Kevin seemed quite excited. 'It's come around again, Uncle B. The Winter Solstice.'

'Sure is, Kevin, and we must do our duty, just as our families have done for centuries. It's what our ancestors did for us and what we are doing now for our descendants.'

'That's right Uncle. I made a promise to continue this rite when you initiated me, and I'll keep it for life.' Kevin was sweating as he said this, despite the cold night air.

'I know you will Kevin, I know. I trust you. But, as I've said before, we must recruit more members from the younger generation. Only from Servion, though. Only Servion.' Balthazar repeated this slowly.

He continued, 'There are just three of us left now, and I'm not going to last forever. Let's now go pick up Cousin Yves at the chapel on the hill. He'll be waiting.'

Kevin drove the fake ambulance slowly up the *Route de Ferlens* then forked right onto the *Route de la Chapelle*. As he braked and brought the van to a halt, he heard a sliding movement in the rear, as if something had bumped up against the doors at the back of the van.

'Shall I go check at the back to see if anything is damaged, Kevin?' Balthazar asked.

'No need. It's probably just an empty food trolly sliding around. Let's enter the chapel now, for the first leg of our ceremony this solstice night.'

Yves Graff, another second cousin of Balthazar and the third and final member of the village solstice sect, greeted them in front of the old wooden oak doors to the chapel. Opening them, all three entered, slowly and in silence.

In his mid-forties, Yves lived alone in the farmhouse on the same dead-end road as the chapel. He managed a herd of twenty-three cows and farmed some arable land scattered across the village. Five years ago, he'd started a side business supplying meat and bones to the Servion zoo. For the lions, tigers, wolves, and boars, mainly. This had now become his main money-spinner. He was now the proud owner of three second-hand industrial freezers located at the back of his farm, where he stored meat he sold on to the zoo.

The original small sixteenth-century chapel had been extended two hundred years ago. Modern stained-glass windows had been fitted more recently. When the new village pastor arrived in the Jorat parish two years ago she'd had most of the old wooden benches removed to free up space for her parish kids' catechism classes. Always good to get them in young, Pastor Véronique Favre had once told Balthazar, not that he was a regular at her Sunday services.

The three began the ritual by donning the red robes Yves stored in the attic of his farm. They then lit the candles which were waxed into ancient sheep skulls fixed firmly onto one-metre-long mahogany sticks.

On each stick was etched the family name of the holder, in this case, the names Bonzon, Gillieron, and Graff, the family names of Balthazar, Kevin, and Yves. In all, Yves stored twenty candlesticks in his attic. On each stick were engraved different names of old Servion families dating back hundreds of years. Nobody knew when the ritual tradition started. The candlesticks had been handed down from father to eldest son from generation to generation.

With only three members left, both Yves and Kevin had asked Balthazar for permission to invite new *non-Servion ancestry* members to join, to which he had replied *over my dead body*. Seeing how Uncle B was shaping up today, Kevin figured that this may not be too long in the future.

Yves then handed out the masks. Like the candlesticks, these had been handed down through many generations. Carved in ebony wood, the masks had probably darkened over time. Glued to the top of each mask were black and white Magpie bird feathers. Cow horns jutted out from the sides and each mask had two old leather straps for attaching to their faces.

Counting down from ten to zero, they all attached their masks in a perfectly synchronized fashion, as if they did this every day. They then started walking slowly around the chapel, red-robed, lit candlesticks in hand, chanting.

Doble, Roble, Moble
Helvétiens avec nous
Doble, Roble, Moble.
Helvétiens avec vous
Doble, Roble, Moble
Ils nous gardent debout

Helvetians are with us.
Helvetians are with you.
And they keep us standing, too.

A call to the spirits of their ancestors perhaps?

At the end of each chant, they paused for a minute and stood in silence, staring almost vacantly down at what appeared to be pre-selected areas of the chapel.

Gravestones underfoot, perhaps?

Then they started moving and chanting again, slowly making their way around the chapel in an anti-clockwise direction.

Having completed three full circles they moved over to the west door, placing their robes and candlesticks into an old leather bag which Yves placed on his lap once inside the ambulance.

Not without a few groans, Balthazar climbed into the ambulance last, with Yves in the middle and Kevin at the wheel. Yves and Balthazar kept their masks on. Kevin had given his to Balthazar, who placed it on his lap for the short journey of the second leg of their solstice trip, the cemetery. The third and final leg would be to the most ancient of local landmarks, the menhir, the standing stone.

It was now 2 a.m. on the night of December 22nd, the winter solstice. As slowly as he could, Kevin drove down the hill, left at the old college, then right, down past the field, and left again past Fabienne Pasche's farmhouse and onto the road leading to the cemetery. The moon was still shining bright.

'How beautiful,' Balthazar whispered to himself, wondering how many more solstice ceremonies he'd lived to celebrate.

Time would tell.

Chapter Eight

Mid-afternoon, Wednesday, December 23, Balthazar's Theatre

As planned, the meeting that Fabienne Pasche had convened began at 3 p.m. the following afternoon at the theatre.

Seated around the table in the foyer were Balthazar, Fabienne Pasche, two men and one woman from the stage crew present the previous evening, and Detective Inspector Philippe Favre. He was doing this as a special treat for Fabienne, an old friend from way back.

Balthazar spoke first.

'Welcome, ladies and gentlemen. Thanks for coming to this debriefing about last night's events. I see that we have Detective Inspector Favre with us today. As one says, we can never be too cautious, but I sincerely hope that we will not be requiring your services any further, detective.'

'So do I Mr. Bonzon,' DI Favre replied. 'It's close to Christmas and the police will be severely tasked, as usual at this time of year. You know, the standard culprits. The partying idiots, the drunk drivers, and the wife-beaters. So, let's keep this debriefing, brief, shall we?'

Fabienne looked at Philippe in complete shock. *He's my friend. He's supposed to be on my side.* Balthazar had a reputation of complete disregard and impertinence for the municipality. When he'd built his new theatre forty years ago, he'd conveniently forgotten to install some obligatory fire doors, which he'd judged unnecessary and far too expensive. The municipality only discovered this omission some years later. They forced him to hire local Servion firefighters at each show until the doors were installed and sent him the bill.

Furious, Balthazar had then sued the council for not having carried out the correct inspections of the new theatre when it was finished. And he won. The village taxpayers were asked to pay. Not only for the installation of the mandatory fire doors but also for hiring the local fire department.

Since that unfortunate episode, any suspicious activity at the theatre was closely scrutinized by the municipality. Detective Inspector Favre's presence today was part of Fabienne Pasche's way of reminding old Balthazar he was not above the law.

'Well, Detective Inspector,' Balthazar replied, 'I could not agree more. So, let's just have a quick round-the-table sum-up and we can all be on our merry ways.'

Balthazar's presence intimidated the stage crew members seated at the bottom end of the table, who remained silent.

Fabienne piped up first. 'Mr. Bonzon, for the record, and you can see that I am recording this meeting with my mobile phone, what were the reasons that forced you to cancel the show at the entr'acte?'

'Weren't you there Mrs. Pasche? There was an electricity outage and we thought there may have been a fire somewhere.'

'That's true, but after five minutes maximum the lights came back on, and the fire department gave you the green light that all was ok. So why not just let the punters back in and re-start the show?'

'Madame la Syndique, you have no idea of how theatre works. The drama, the tension, and the excitement of the show had been lost by the time we got the okay to carry on. We'd have never got the same level of dramaturgy back had the punters returned. In any case, there were still technical problems, weren't there?'

Balthazar looked to the three stage crew members for support. A hesitant voice – a woman's – from the crew member was heard.

'It wasn't us, boss. Sorry.'

'Speak up,' replied Balthazar, 'we can't hear you at this end of the table, especially with all the actors prancing in and out of here as if they owned the place.'

Balthazar shouted across the foyer. 'Will everyone please be quiet! That's better. Now, what did you say again my little woman?'

The woman in question, who was not little at all, stood up and repeated. 'It wasn't us; it was Kevin.'

'What wasn't you?'

'We did not mess with the electric box. Kevin oversaw that yesterday evening. We know he doesn't do this normally, and we were also surprised that you'd mandated him to do this on your stage instructions, boss.'

Balthazar was suddenly both motionless and speechless, trying to remember if he'd done that, or not.

'Don't worry. I'm not going to bite your heads off. Yes, of course, it was me, I remember now. I asked Kevin to manage the curtains and the electricity box, you're right,' Balthazar did not sound convincing.

Observing Balthazar's reaction, DI Favre's interest was aroused. Was his old copper's nose spotting a lie? Maybe.

'Mr. Bonzon, why isn't Kevin here this afternoon? Are you wasting my time? If I have any use whatsoever, it's to give some advice to all of you so that this matter can be cleared up as quickly as possible. Now you tell me that the person who caused all this is not even here! That is not very professional of you.'

'I'm sorry, Detective. As Mrs. Pasche knows very well, Kevin Gillieron is employed full-time by the municipality, the one that she heads, here in Servion. He only works now and again at my theatre. He'll be at the municipal recycling centre now. He manages the trash tip for Servion and the next-door village. They've even got CCTV there now. Changed from I was a kid. He's there most days from three until five. Surprised that Madame la Syndique hasn't told you that already.'

Detective Inspector Favre stood up and asked Fabienne Pasche for a quiet word, asking the others to remain seated at the table. A few minutes later the two returned to the table.

In his strong, firm, and authoritative voice, DI Favre summarised the situation.

'The Syndique, Mrs. Pasche, will be writing a short, factual report about the unfortunate events yesterday evening. There is no need to worry, Mr. Bonzon, you and your team will not in any way be blamed. We will need to speak with Kevin Gillieron to find out exactly what happened to the electrics. But there is no hurry, and we will do that after the Christmas festivities. Thank you for your time, and a Merry Christmas to all!'

The stage crew returned backstage and Balthazar to his office. As the Syndique and DI Favre were approaching the exit door of the foyer, a shortish, pretty young woman who Favre recognized straightway was walking in, hurriedly, with intent. It was his intern at police headquarters, that annoying Criminology Ph.D. candidate, Marianne Devaud.

'Detective Inspector. I called on Pastor Favre at your house and she told me you'd be here. It's my brother Dani. The football player. He's

29

been missing since last night. And something inside tells me he's dead. Dead. Dead. Tell me this cannot be happening, please.'

Thinking quickly on his feet, Favre grabbed Marianne by the arm and told her they were going back to Mézières together, now. They'd go to his and his wife's home to discuss this in a calm and collected manner, as was his way. No need to panic. This sort of thing happens all the time. Dani will surely return soon.

Leaving the theatre, he informed his friend the Syndique that he'd come around to her house later and that this whole matter was probably just a village storm in a village teacup.

Chapter Nine

Late afternoon, Wednesday, December 23, Pastor Favre's Residence, Mézières

The resident protestant pastor of the Evangelical Reformed Church in Mézières lived in a large building adjacent to the temple constructed in 1707.

Protestantism was declared the official religion in Vaud Canton at the beginning of the Reformation in the 16th century. The Geneva icon Jean Calvin himself, no less, was present at the Notre Dame cathedral in Lausanne when this had happened five hundred years ago. And ever since, the protestant church and the salaries of its pastors have been paid by the canton's taxpayers.

Philippe Favre asked Marianne Devaud to sit in the back of his car for the five-minute trip on the old, straight, raised Roman road to his house. Or more precisely, his *wife's* house in Mézières, where they lived there rent-free, though a nominal amount was docked from Véronique Favre's salary each month.

'Mr. Favre, Sir, why did you ask me to sit in the back?' Marianne asked, without wanting to cause a scene.

'Never you mind young lady. None of your business. Put your seat belt on. You studied criminology. You should know that most accidents happen less than five minutes from home.'

Favre had been the driver in a fatal accident when he was just eighteen. It was not his fault. A truck pulled out at speed from a side road and hit his flimsy Fiat Panda full-on, instantly killing his girlfriend, who was in the passenger seat. He'd only been slightly injured and had felt survivor's guilt for years. Since then, nobody had ever been allowed to sit in the front passenger seat of a car Favre drove, even his fellow police officers.

Detective Inspector Favre was now driving at speed towards Mézières, well above the limit. Just before the village, he slammed on the brakes. Seated in the back, Marianne was relieved she'd fastened her belt. Deep in his thoughts about the whole strange theatre incident the night before, Favre had almost forgotten about the speed trap at the entrance to Mézières. The revenue from that trap must have paid his salary a few times over. At the cantonal Police HQ, they had annual bets on which speed trap would make the most money for the canton, and this one in Mézières regularly came out on top.

Favre slammed on the brakes and entered the village driving well below the limit, as if to make a point, Favre drove his twelve-year-old Opel Antara slowly over the speed bump, past the bakery and right onto the parking area in front of the church, and over to the front door of his wife's official residence.

'Come on in Marianne. Véronique asked your mother round as well.'

Whether it was the lure of home or the fact that he was on revered ground, Favre suddenly seemed warmer and softer as he escorted Marianne into a very large living room. It was the first time she'd been inside the mansion, and she guessed that this room was used for pastoral work by Pastor Véronique. Her mother and the Pastor were talking politely, seated around a table that could've hosted twelve parishioners or more. They'd already had coffee and the remainders of a cake were left on a plate.

'None left for us, my sweet?' Philippe inquired, with eyes like a dog waiting for his dinner.

So, there is a softer side to that harsh and unwelcoming front Favre projects constantly, Marianne thought. Véronique went to get some more coffee and cakes in the adjacent kitchen, which also appeared too big and industrial for a couple.

'Mrs. Devaud. Very nice to see you again. Now tell me what your cause of concern is and how I can help.' Philippe's voice was somewhat condescending, and he spoke slowly and loudly as if he'd expected Mrs. Devaud not to fully understand the French language.

Marianne butted straight in. 'When I came home this morning to say goodbye to Dani before he flew back to England, I was surprised to find…'

'Yes, you've told me all that Marianne, no need to repeat. I'd like to have your mother's side of the story. Mrs. Devaud?' DI Favre was insistent.

Had Detective Inspector Favre not been a high-up policeman in the service that was presently employing her as an intern for her doctoral thesis, Marianne would have let rip. Wisely, she zipped it, almost biting her tongue in the process.

'Many thanks for hearing us out, Detective Inspector,' said Mrs. Devaud, with only a very tiny hint of a foreign accent. 'I don't want to trouble the police with all this. Especially at this time of the year. And I know that my daughter constantly worries about her brother Dani. It should be the other way around. After all, he's the older one. She's right, he didn't come home last night. And yes, I was a bit worried about that message on his phone. But I know my Dani. He's always joking around. Wouldn't surprise me if he walked straight in here right now and laughed his head off seeing Marianne's surprise and anger. I'm sure he'll turn up sooner or later, safe and sound.'

'I think you're right Mrs. Devaud,' Favre replied, in a less disdainful voice this time.

'No, he won't, and neither will Marco Zurcher. They're dead, I'm sure of it.' interrupted Marianne 'And if nobody else is going to do anything, I'll find out myself where they are and who killed them.'

Philippe Favre was almost indignant. 'For a Ph.D. candidate in Criminology, Miss Devaud, that's some wild statement.'

'Well, for a supposed Detective Inspector responsible for solving crime in this canton, I cannot believe how lightly you are taking this case.'

Favre took his time before replying.

'Ok, I'll get some staff on it. But if it turns out we're wasting valuable police time at such a busy time of year, you may have to find another police force for your Ph.D. Miss Devaud.'

Marianne realized that she'd probably overstepped the mark. 'Sorry sir,' she spurted. 'I'm just upset and worried.'

Favre continued.

'Firstly, we've got to find out what happened to Marco Zurcher. And that, Marianne, is going to be your job. Do you want to work on a real case if this turns out to be one? Now's your chance. Show me what you're made of. Off you go now. Meet me tomorrow morning in my office. 7.30 a.m. sharp.'

So early, thought Marianne?

Marianne was not a morning person at all. She'd once done an internet search for jobs for night owls, and *police officer* had come up in the top ten. But that was deceptive, as most police officers also had to be early birds for the morning shifts. They had to be adaptable to all hours. Did she really want this line of work? First, finish the Criminology

PhD and then decide. The police rarely took doctoral interns, and she realized she was lucky to have landed this internship.

After several weeks working with DI Favre, Marianne was still trying to figure out his hot and cold, open and then closed attitude and behaviour. She'd already seen him a few times in action in the office, when he addressed his team in the same condescending manner he used with her mother. It was almost arrogant, but not quite. Something was missing. Then again, how to explain that warm tinge of softness and generosity when he showed her into his home?

As she left the house, she realized she'd need to find out more about the enigmatic DI Favre.

Back at her mother's apartment, Marianne called Marco's parents, who had moved back to Luzern, in the Swiss-German part of the country. They had not heard from Marco for some time and were not even aware he'd attended the football club fund-raiser at the theatre. Marianne did not mention to Marco's parents the text message she'd received from Dani. No need to upset them. Not yet at least.

Additional calls confirmed that Marco had recently split up with his girlfriend, who did not have any idea where he was, and really couldn't care. The cheating bastard.

Which left just one option. Marianne would have to ask DI Favre to authorize a search of Marco Zurcher's penthouse apartment down by the lakeside. Quickly.

Chapter Ten

Early evening, Wednesday, December 23, Philippe's renovated farmhouse, Chemin du Cimetière

Once Marianne had left, Favre jumped back into his old motor and speeded back down the straight road to Servion. He was emotionally attached to his car. A mate, who was a car salesman, told him the nickname for Opel in the trade was *Poubelle*. It rhymed well. Favre liked that description and had called his Opel *La Poubelle* ever since. He'd never had any problem with his *Poubelle* and, as there weren't many of them around, could always spot it a mile away. It was unique. Why change?

Fabienne was expecting him. She'd laid out a traditional Vaudois aperitif: local Chasselas white wine from Lutry; dried and thinly sliced beef and pork meats from the Gros-de-Vaud region; different local cheeses, including the famous *Brigands du Jorat* cheese named after an infamous gang of impoverished outlaws who used to ambush convoys traveling through the local woods back in the eighteenth century.

After some small talk and a glass of wine, Philippe got down to business.

'No love lost between you and old Balthazar I see, Fabienne?'

'No kidding, Philippe. Behind that friendly, thespian smile and laugh, the man's a paranoid psycho. A total control freak and a misogynist to boot. The man thinks he owns the village. Oh, and by the way, he's up to his old tricks again with those solstice fanatics. I saw them again last night.'

'Solstice fanatics?' Philippe asked, not knowing about this tradition in the village.

'I've never told you about the solstice group, have I? It's an old tradition. Nobody seems to know when it started. At each solstice, the men in the old Servion families honour the dead. Past midnight, a procession takes place from the chapel, down to the cemetery, and over to the menhir.'

Philippe was listening, very attentively.

'And what do they do?'

'Apparently, they chant some gobbledegook rhyme, wearing some old dusty robes and crazy masks, and wander around each site

35

communicating with the dead, ending up at the menhir. Harmless, as far as I'm concerned, but not my thing. Little-by-little most families left the solstice group. I'm not too sure how many are now left. Can't be many.'

'Why the menhir?' asked Philippe.

'Good question. The solstice sect claim that their family ancestors have been around since the bronze age, five thousand years ago. Most people didn't believe this until they discovered the menhir in 1996. They dug it out and stood it up. Which, I guess, proved them right, somehow.'

Philippe was visibly fascinated by these old village stories.

Fabienne continued. 'A village rumour, passed down through at least a couple of generations, says that somewhere around the menhir are buried a young woman and a young man who lived together on the same farm. They died in suspicious circumstances. But no one knows which farm, or how they died.'

'Would they not have found their bones when they excavated the menhir?' Philippe asked.

'Apparently not.'

'And Kevin Gillieron, the municipal employee. How is he connected to this?'

'There is another rumour only a few people in the village know. That Kevin's father was the son of siblings who lived on a farm near the menhir.'

'You mean...' said Philippe, clearly shocked.

'Yes, I do mean that, and Kevin's dad was born nine months later.'

'Hmm.' Philippe didn't seem convinced.

'Surely that sort of thing was no longer happening at that time. It was not very long ago, Fabienne. Kevin's dad is how old?'

'He's dead.' Fabienne replied.

'He committed suicide ten years ago. Maybe he discovered the truth about his parents? Nobody seems to know the full story. Balthazar has been a surrogate father to Kevin ever since.'

'And his parents, the alleged siblings?'

'Nobody knows. They disappeared from the face of the earth when the dad was born. He was adopted. No idea how the rumour of incest ever surfaced.'

'Ok,' Philippe said. 'But what has all this got to do with the solstice group? And I thought we were here to talk about the events of last night at the theatre and the subsequent disappearance of Dani Devaud and Marc Zurcher.'

Fabienne was on a roll

'Let me explain the connection, my dear Detective Inspector. When Kevin drove past here, he was at the wheel of the *same ambulance* we saw on stage at the theatre. With two other people in the front of the vehicle wearing those crazy solstice masks.'

She continued. 'It must've been around 2 a.m. I'm a light sleeper, as you know. I was looking out of the bedroom window. That same ambulance came past. No mistaking. With Kevin at the wheel. No headlights. Moving slowly. They stopped at the cemetery, and I saw three figures walk slowly in, with lit candles. Could not identify them, apart from Kevin, who I'd seen at the wheel.'

Philippe was beginning to wonder if this had anything to do with the disappearance of Dani and Marco. His mind was racing. But he didn't want to voice his thoughts out loud. No. That would be far too unprofessional in the presence of Fabienne, even if the two had shared an intimate connection in the past. He had now built a wonderful, loving relationship with his wife Véronique and did not want to spoil it. And he was very aware of his weaknesses in the presence of Fabienne.

Fabienne carried on. 'After fifteen minutes, they all got back into the car and carried on towards the menhir.'

Philippe interrupted. 'How do you know they were going to the menhir, Fabienne?'

'Where else would they be going? I bet if you check with the old woman at the farm up there on the hill, she'll confirm my supposition. She's got a great view of the menhir from her front room. And she's a real night owl, along with her pet wolves she keeps in her back garden.'

'She keeps wolves?' asked Philippe, incredulously.

'Yeah. It's not illegal to keep wolves. Philippe. Listen to me. I'm not suggesting anything untoward was going on last night other than some crazy, druid ancestor worship ritual, but why were the using the same mock ambulance that was on stage?'

'OK, Fabienne. I'll call Balthazar right now, this minute, to check. Do you have his number?'

Philippe called from her phone.

Balthazar answered immediately. 'Madame *le*, or should I say *la* Syndique. How can I be of help? Want me to pay more taxes, perhaps?'

Philippe's voice changed dramatically from the old friend in the living room with Fabienne, to the professional police officer.

'Good evening, Mr. Bonzon. Sorry to bother you. This is Detective Inspector Philippe Favre. We have reason to believe that Kevin Gillieron was driving a car belonging to your theatre at around 2 p.m. earlier this morning, with two passengers who had their faces covered with strange masks. Can you confirm the disappearance of the mock ambulance that was used on stage yesterday evening?'

Balthazar did not reply straight away.

'Are you still there Mr. Bonzon?' Philippe asked.

'Yes, yes, of course. No, Detective Inspector. There is no problem. The vehicle was in our car park, with its refrigerated compartment hooked up to the mains, charging all night.'

'Would you mind if I sent an officer over to check the CCTV cameras in the car park?'

'Not at all, Detective Inspector. But your officer won't find anything as my CCTV has been out of order since the outage last night. I'm getting it fixed tomorrow.'

'OK, Mr. Bonzon. Thanks very much for your help and have a merry Christmas.'

Philippe handed the phone back to Fabienne, saying he'd better be getting back home. It was a busy time of year for Véronique, and he'd promised to cook dinner. He said he'd be in touch soon and wished her all the best for the festive season.

As soon as he'd finished the call with DI Favre, Balthazar called his second cousin.

'Kevin. It's me. You must come to the theatre, immediately. Something's up and we need to fix it. Now, before it's too late.'

Chapter Eleven

Later that evening, Wednesday, December 23, at 9 p.m., Balthazar's office, Balthazar's theatre,

'About time Kevin. Where the hell have you been?' Balthazar screamed, face red with rage.

'Just finished at the dump, Uncle B. What's up?'

Kevin removed his bright, orange-coloured work vest and took a seat opposite Balthazar in his office. The adjustable study chair he sat on was fixed at a low height, forcing him to look up towards Uncle B, who suddenly appeared even more daunting than usual.

'That annoying policeman DI Favre just called me. On Fabienne Pasche's phone. Seems they are closer than I'd thought.'

'And…'

'And, Kevin, our dear lady Syndique said she saw *you* driving the stage ambulance towards the cemetery last night. Luckily Yves and I had our masks on.'

Kevin was determined, for once, not to be intimidated.

'Is that a problem? Live and let live, that's what I say. No crime in following our ancestral traditions and respecting our elders on the solstice. You told me that many times.'

'That's not the issue here, Kevin. What worries me is that Favre will start to get the wrong end of the stick. Not your fault, I suppose, you weren't there when that rude young woman Marianne Devaud interrupted our meeting yesterday claiming her brother Dani had been killed?'

Kevin was shocked. 'Dani Devaud, dead?'

'Well, there's no evidence of anything. Just that Marianne has not had any news from Dani since the theatre evacuation yesterday.'

'No problem then. He'll turn up,' Kevin said, almost disappointingly.

'And if he doesn't? If he is dead? And if Favre is thinking that you are somehow connected to his murder? I should have checked that bumping noise in the back of the van last night. Kevin, are you hiding something from me?'

'Uncle B, I think you're overly dramatizing things, as you sometimes can. And that's not a compliment, and not a joke, either.'

'Look, Kevin. I may be old and decrepit. But I'm no fool. I remember all those problems you had with Dani at school. And if my memory is correct, Marco Zurcher taunted you as well, didn't he?'

As Balthazar said this, Kevin put his head in his hands and almost started to cry.

'Kevin. Listen to me. Dani and Marco are assholes. What they said about your father is not true. All that taunting you at school. Your dad's parents – your grandparents - were *not* brother and sister. They were not siblings. They were not even related. I know that *for sure*. It's an ugly rumour that's been going around this village for far too long now.'

Kevin looked up. 'Then why did my dad commit suicide?'

This time it was Balthazar's turn to put his head in his hands.

'Please, tell me, Uncle B. I need to know.'

'And there's something I need to know as well,' Balthazar said, deflecting Kevin's question.

'You must tell me the truth now Kevin. Was it Marco and Dani in that ambulance last night? Was it their dead bodies bumping around in the back? Did you kill them, Kevin? What did you do with their bodies?'

'No, no, I'd never do a thing like that. You know I wouldn't. Please.'

Balthazar thought for a moment.

'Kevin. It'll be fine. Don't worry. I'll sort it out. Blood is thicker than water. We're in this together.'

'But, but....' Kevin said, with tears rolling down his cheek.

'No buts, no ifs, no nothing. Go home, Kevin. Get some rest. Your Uncle B will not betray you. You have my full support. We'll get through this. But you must always, always, tell me the truth.'

With that, Balthazar got up, hugged Kevin, who was now sobbing non-stop, and guided him without any further conversation out of the theatre to his car, arm around his shoulder.

'It's ok. If you go to prison, we'll get you out. You can count on your old Uncle B.'

Chapter Twelve

The next day, December 24, 7 a.m. DI Favre's office, Vaud Police HQ, La Blécherette, Lausanne

Marianne had been up all night trying to find out as much she could about Philippe Favre. She'd surprised herself with what she'd uncovered. She'd used a series of search engines, *LinkedIn*, and analyzed data from different social media platforms. Crazy how many people, including many of Favre's friends and acquaintances, left the access to their profiles wide open for anyone to see.

She arrived at the Police HQ on the outskirts of Lausanne, just next to the *autoroute* at La Blécherette, at 7 a.m. before Favre, for once. The building was non-descript. Concrete and windows. Nothing out of the ordinary. The Swiss and Vaudois flags were waving high in the wind on their poles on the top of the building. A couple of police vans were parked outside the front and a few more behind the back. The building was on the *Chemin de la lanterne*. Marianne hoped the police would be able to shed some light on the disappearance of her brother.

She had been given a permanent badge to enter the office the previous week by her direct superior, whom herself reported to Favre. The badge allowed her access to certain, but not all areas of the building.

For her six-month internship, she'd been allocated a fixed office cubicle in an open-space area near Favre's closed and Venetian-blinded office.

What had she found out so far about Philippe Favre from her internet research?

On the historical archive site of the Evangelical Reformed Church of Vaud Canton website, she'd come across an article recounting the tragic death in South Africa of Danielle Favre, wife of missionary Etienne Favre, and mother of Philippe Thabiso Favre.

Judging from the date, this happened when Favre was twelve years old. Interesting. His father was a protestant Pastor, like the woman he'd married. His mother had died tragically when he was young, like his first girlfriend. Marianne had also looked up the origin of the name Thabiso, which meant *Joy*. Looked like Favre had not had that much joy in his early life, and it had deeply affected him.

His father had been a missionary for many years in different locations in Botswana, Africa. The family had moved four or five times there and only returned to Switzerland after his wife's death.

From the age of twelve, Favre had done his schooling in Yverdon and joined the Swiss army for his military service at eighteen. After his obligatory four months of training, he'd been selected for the officer corps and had done many additional, non-obligatory stints since then. Philippe Favre had risen to the grade of Sergeant-Major, quite a high level in the Swiss military.

Marianne wondered whether the turbulence of his earlier existence had made Favre seek out the stability, security, and regularity he'd found, firstly with the army and now with the police.

At her desk that early morning, her PC was open on a news item about Favre she'd just found.

Military conscript denies responsibility for girlfriend's death

The headline from the daily newspaper *24 Heures* was on Marianne's screen when DI Favre appeared, out of nowhere, behind her.

'That was a long time ago Marianne. And I was exonerated in case you were wondering. What news of Marco Zurcher?'

Marianne stuttered, 'I'm very sorry sir. I wasn't…'

'News of Marco Zurcher?'

Marianne steadied her nerves. She was fully aware that DI Favre was giving her a massive chance to prove herself in this case.

'I called his parents, sir, and they haven't had any news from him for some time. The concierge of Marc's penthouse apartment in Lutry told me the lights were off and he hadn't seen any activity since Wednesday afternoon. Marco's girlfriend, or should I say his ex, told me he was a cheating bastard, and she couldn't care less.'

'Does she still have the keys to Zurcher's apartment?'

'Sorry, sir, I didn't ask her that.'

'Marianne, if we are to work together you have to stop saying sorry.'

'Sorry, sir, I won't say it anymore. Should I ask her for the keys, sir?'

Favre was a morning person and was thinking clearly

'It would certainly help if she had the keys, yes. When we search the premises, it will make things easier. Of course, the concierge may also have a key. We'll see.'

'That's what I think we should do as well.'

'Then it looks like I'll have to formally open a *Missing Persons* case for Mr. Dani Devaud and Mr. Marco Zurcher.'

Marianne felt like jumping out of her seat and giving DI Favre a big hug and a kiss. She didn't.

'Should we also get in touch with Dirk de Clippele, sir?'

'Who? And, by the way, you don't have to call me *sir* all the time. Marianne. Only when other officers are around, thanks.'

'Understood, sir. Dirk de Clippele is the football agent of Marco, Dani, and Granit Berisha.'

'Granit Berisha?' Favre replied. He then quickly corrected himself, so as not to appear stupid. 'Of course, Granit Berisha. Liverpool FC, yes?'

Marianne instantly clicked that Philippe Favre was not a football fan and had not been paying much attention at the fund-raising show the other evening.

'Do you think this Dirk de Clippele is important in this whole business, Marianne'

'Dani thinks the world of him. These football agents are often like an extended family to the players they manage. If anyone knows where Marco and Dani are, it would be Dirk. I should have called him earlier in fact. Stupid me.'

'You do that, and I'll open the *Mispers* file. And get what we know so far down on paper. You should be good at that, being a Ph.D. student, and all that.'

'Will do.'

'Let's catch up at lunch. There's a place close by we can eat.'

Marianne felt elated. Maybe she should become a morning person after all. What was that saying? *The early bird gets the worm.* That's the one. Or in this case, the lunch. She was beginning to warm to him, despite his austere and rigid exterior.

Marianne spent the rest of the morning penning the report. It took five calls to Dirk de Clippele's reply message before he picked up. And that was only after Marianne had texted him saying that her brother was missing.

The conversation with de Clippele was short and to the point. No, he did not know that Marco and Dani had gone missing. Yes, he had seen them get up from the stage after the lights went out and move towards to backstage exit. No, he didn't have any plans to speak to them soon. And yes, he was very busy, so he'd have to leave it at that.

At midday they left for lunch. Little had Marianne realized that Philippe Favre was an even quicker food eater than he was a car driver. She'd sat in the *back* of the Opel *Poubelle*, now understanding *why*, for the five-minute speed drive to the restaurant in Le-Mont-sur-Lausanne. The whole outing had taken less than forty-five minutes. Over the meal, she'd briefed him on Dirk de Clippele's non-committal replies. Favre had calmly explained they'd have to be patient before making any real progress on this case, whether Dani and Marco were dead, missing, or just messing around.

In the car, on the way back Favre asked Marianne for any ideas for a nice present for his wife. Bloody cheek, she thought! Véronique could be twice her age. Biting her tongue once again, she recommended a very expensive perfume brand that she'd never use herself. Favre was happy. He dropped her off at the office, wished her a Merry Christmas, and headed into town to buy a very expensive brand of perfume.

Chapter Thirteen

Monday morning, December 28

Christmas comes and goes. Too quickly for many, but not quickly enough for others.

Véronique Favre was happy and satisfied with the success of her festive season's services at the temple in Mézières. Christmas worshippers were always more numerous than on other holy days, except for Easter Sunday. And the donation collection had been good. In her sermon, she'd encouraged her congregation to marvel at the beauty and innocence of the baby Jesus. To focus on the beauty of new life. On renewal.

Philippe Favre had become a little jaded with his parents' religion over the years. He described himself as a sincere believer and follower of the fundamental teachings of Jesus, but not of the *whole Christianity construct*. His words. Despite his misgivings, he always supported his wife in her role as Pastor.

Monday morning had come around too quickly for Véronique, but not for Philippe. Always the early bird, he was in his office by 7.30 a.m. This time, Marianne had beaten him to it. The two of them were drinking a coffee at the machine when Favre's phone pinged. It was Fabienne Pasche.

'Madame *la* Syndique,' Favre said imitating Balthazar, 'what can I do for you, my dear?' Marianne was surprised. The man does have a sense of humour then.

'It's serious, Philippe. Get to the theatre as quickly as you can. It's old Balthazar. He's been found dead by one of the cleaning staff in his office. Looks like he's been dead for a couple of days.'

'How do you know that Fabienne? Don't touch anything! Don't move anything! Don't let the cleaner go anywhere! Nor anyone else who's present. We'll be there in twenty minutes. As will forensics.'

Favre ran back to his office, grabbed his bag, and got Marianne to call the lift. But it was blocked somewhere on floor three. The two ran down the fire escape stairs to the underground car park where Favre's Opel Antara was parked. Marianne did not wait for instructions, jumping directly into the back. Favre took the wheel and sped out of the parking at well above the ten-kilometer limit.

On his way out of the garage, he put a special magnetic flasher on the roof of the car and turned on his siren. Marianne had never ridden in an improvised police car with the siren screaming, and lights blazing. Favre took the back roads directly to Servion, east via Chalet-à-Gobet, then through the Jorat forest. Marianne checked her *Maps* App on her smartphone. It would take around twenty-eight minutes via this route to get to Servion. They arrived after twenty-one minutes.

Fabienne was waiting for them at the entrance to the theatre.

'This way. Follow me,'

To Marianne's amazement, forensics had beaten them and were already on site.

They got to Balthazar's office, where two forensic experts, a woman and a man, were already attending to the body. Balthazar was in his study chair, with his head slumped on the table. His right arm was underneath his chest, with his hand clutching his chest. The two experts explained they were not going to move the body for some time, as they must do a series of tests beforehand.

The woman, who appeared to know Favre well, explained her initial impressions directly to Favre as if Fabienne and Marianne were invisible.

'Looks like a heart attack to me Philippe. We'll do an autopsy, of course. I think we can rule out any foul play. I'll get the full report emailed to you by Wednesday at the latest. Meantime, get yourselves into protective gear and you can begin your work. Here's his iPhone.'

Favre thanked them. Minutes later he and Marianne returned to the office and proceeded to do their examination. Not of Balthazar's dead body, with his eyes still open, but of his office.

Favre opened Balthazar's computer, and, to his amazement, there was no password required. Marianne wondered whether this was standard police practice and whether she should say anything, but her curiosity got the better of her.

'What are you looking for Philippe?' she asked.

'Ideally, I'd like to find the code for his mobile phone. Maybe he noted it down somewhere on his PC?'

'Sounds too easy to me. Would you do that?'

46

'No, but he was over eighty, and most people that age are not the geeky type. Marianne, go through the filing cabinet and drawers to see what you can dig up. And give me some ideas for a password a bigmouth like Balthazar would use for his phone.'

While this was happening, the forensic experts were still poking around, doing what they do. Marianne thought she was in a TV series.

After ten minutes Philippe piped up again. 'What about *Thespian*? Could that be his phone password Marianne? There is a digital file here called *Great Thespians of Switzerland*. In it are subfiles. And guess what name is at the top? You've got it, Balthazar!'

Marianne had not found anything in the drawers or the filing cabinet. Then again, she didn't know what she should be looking for, and Favre had given her no guidance.

'We have a maximum of three tries on an iPhone, and then it blocks. In my criminology studies, I've learned it's often very simple. What was the name of his mother? And what date was he born?'

'Ask Fabienne. She's outside.'

Five minutes later Marianne returned with the name and the date.

'Which one shall I try first, boss?' Somehow *boss* resonated better than *sir*, now that they had become better acquainted.

'Mother's name,' Favre replied.

Marianne had to be very attentive typing it in, as each number on the phone, apart from the number one, referenced three letters. Two was ABC. Three was DEF, and so on. She had to translate each letter into a number. The mother's name had six letters, as is required by an iPhone code. So far so good. J E A N N E.

It didn't work.

Two attempts remained before the phone would block.

'OK, forget *Thespian*, try his birth date, month, and year,' Favre said.

Marianne did this, with the utmost attention.

It didn't work.

Marianne had an idea. What if old Balthazar were more tech-savvy than Favre had assumed?

She pointed the phone towards the dead face of Balthazar. *Hey presto!* It worked. Facial recognition.

'Done it, boss. I managed to open the phone and I've changed the code. Here's the new one: 123456. Don't think we'll forget that one, will we?'

'Good work Marianne. Give me the phone.'

Marianne once again felt elated. She'd been smart. Smarter than her boss. And she'd not winced once at the sight of her first dead body, though she did feel like retching.

With Balthazar's phone in hand, Favre asked Marianne to accompany her out of the office where they found Fabienne.

'We need a private place to listen to the messages on his phone, Fabienne,'

Fabienne said they could use her office at the Servion municipal building, the old primary school, just up the street.

Inside Fabienne's office, Favre and Marianne proceeded to listen, via the speakerphone, to all the stored voicemails. They also read all the text messages on Balthazar's phone. It was a tedious process that took over two hours. And there was nothing of interest. Marianne then scoured Balthazar's email. Nothing of importance.

Frustrated, Favre gave Marianne the phone saying he needed coffee, and left the room.

Marianne opened the phone and looked at the apps. It's a long shot, she thought, but what the hell? The *Voice Memo* App! Let's give it a try. She opened the app and saw just one recording, from the previous Wednesday evening, 9.36 p.m. She clicked on the link and listened to it. It was a recording of the conversation Balthazar had had with Kevin Gillieron that evening.

She listened to the recording three times. And each time Balthazar's question on the recording kept coming back to her.

Tell me the truth now Kevin. Was it Marco and Dani in that ambulance last night? Was it their dead bodies bumping around in the back? Did you kill them, Kevin? What did you do with their bodies?

Tears filled her eyes. She told herself to remain professional. She waited until her hands had stopped trembling. Got up. Went out of the door of Fabienne's office and said: 'Boss, come quickly. You need to hear this. I think we've found Dani and Marco's killer.'

PART TW0

THE *BRIO TRIO* RISE TO FAME

FIFTEEN YEARS AGO

Chapter Fourteen

FIFTEEN YEARS AGO
FC Jorat Mézières football ground, Vaud Canton, Switzerland

Mr. Dirk de Clippele was finally here. Attending a football match on FC Jorat Mézières' sacred turf. Up until that point Coach Weymo had been dealing with the Belgian's sub-agents in Switzerland, who had all guaranteed that the *Brio Trio* – Granit Berisha, Dani Devaud, and Marco Zurcher - would be taken under the great Dirk de Clippele's wings. The future for them was bright. They would be signed immediately for Lausanne Sports where they'd surely improve quickly in the team's Academy.

Unfortunately, Kevin Gillieron had not made the cut; he was not good enough. Shame, thought *Weymo*, but what the hell; three of his youngsters from the same year on their way to becoming professionals was quite an achievement. And his financial reward would last a lifetime, with a percentage of their earnings right up to the end of their careers. Not that this was strictly legal, mind. UEFA regulations did not allow that. Then again, a contract was a contract, UEFA, or no UEFA. And the one he'd made with Dirk should generate enough regular income for him to finally buy that house in the village. This agreement remained a secret between the two. No one else knew.

Kevin Gillieron, though, would remain an amateur. Weymo promised to make him captain as consolation once the *Trio* has moved over to Lausanne Sports FC. This should also make up for all the nasty comments Kevin had been getting from Dani and Marco. Something to do with incest, apparently. Strange, weird Servion village gossip thought *Weymo*. Then again, no worse than in his native Scotland.

The match kicked off at 1 p.m. *Weymo's* thirteen-year-olds were playing Fribourg FC, a much bigger team from a big city, but *Weymo* was not worried. He knew his team would win. They always did.

Dirk's black, chauffeur-driven Mercedes pulled up in the parking lot in front of the small FC Jorat Mézières clubhouse. Was it a bullet-proof car? As the chauffeur got out, *Weymo* wondered if Dirk had hired him from the Belgian secret service or the local boxing club. All neck and shoulders. Crew-cut and shades. Not exactly your average limo chauffeur. He knew that Dirk was worth a pretty penny or two, but was this necessary? In little hometown Mézières?

The chauffeur opened the left back door and out stepped Dirk de Clippele. He walked confidently towards *Weymo*. Out of the other door, a very beautiful, expensively dressed woman followed behind Dirk.

Dirk spoke in a perfect Queen's English, the sort that very few English people use today. 'Mr. Ray McCauley. Dirk de Clippele. Finally, we get to meet. Honoured. And this is my lawyer and confidante-in-chief, Anita Patel, from London.'

Dirk's neatly styled hair and muscular, toned body contrasted sharply with *Weymo*'s long, wavy and somewhat unkempt red hair, and his well-nourished beer belly.

'Very pleased to meet you, Mr. de Clippele, as well as you, of course, Mrs. Patel. Call me *Weymo*. Everyone does around here.'

Dirk loosened his iron-fisted grip. 'Can't wait to see our little geniuses in action, *Weymo*. Please call us Dirk and Anita. As Anita mentioned on the phone, we don't want to talk with any of the players' parents. Not today, at any rate. That's your job. You're our intermediary, our liaison officer, if you will. We aim to remain incognito this afternoon if you don't mind?'

Coach Weymo suppressed the laughter that was on its way up. *Incognito*? Here at our little village ground in Mézières? With that car? And that gorilla hovering over the two of them constantly? You must be kidding!

'Of course, Dirk. We'll take care of it. Let me show you to the stands.'

Weymo took the three of them around the back of the clubhouse onto what was not really a football stand, more a set of chairs arranged haphazardly on some steps next to the pitch. They'd watch the game *incognito* from there.

At the end of the match, the coach of FC Fribourg was furious, complaining profusely to the referee about an offside on goal number two. He'd underestimated FC Jorat Mézières today. Had nobody told him? He should have done his homework. The small team's thirteen-year-olds had already beaten the equivalent, big city Geneva and Lausanne teams, home and away. At six goals to one, this was FC Fribourg's biggest defeat of the season. Granit Berisha had scored four of those goals and Dani Devaud and Marco Zurcher had five assists between them. The other two goals had been scored by Kevin Gillieron, ever the workhorse.

Weymo escorted Dirk and Anita back to their car. Everyone was watching him and his two guests. *What was Weymo up to?* He knew he'd have to work out some valid explanation to his players' parents for next week's match. He'd figure it out.

As they said goodbye, Dirk was all smiles. This time the smiles seemed genuine. 'That was magic, *Weymo*, pure magic. My Swiss agents were right, and so were you. Three very promising young soccer players, with Granit the clear leader of the pack. We'll all be in the money with these three, my friend. Big time, I hope. I'm going to call them the *Brio Trio*. Sounds good, no? Anita will get back to you ASAP. And please, no need to talk to UEFA or anyone else.'

Weymo said goodbye and pondered on what Dirk had said about the UEFA rules and regulations. UEFA – the Union of European Football Associations – had strict rules governing the financial management by agents of *professional* football players. Very true. But the *Brio Trio* were still kids, nowhere near professional yet. So, we'll cross that bridge when we get there, thought *Weymo*.

He got into his old Citroen BX and headed home to give the good news to his wife and kids that they'd soon be able to buy that house they'd always wanted in Servion. But he'd never explain how.

Chapter Fifteen

TEN YEARS AGO,

Sitges, Spain, European Under 18 Football Championship

It was day five of the month-long tournament. The Swiss under-18 national team had taken up residence at the Hotel Splendid in the town of Sitges, located in the Catalan region of Spain. Most of their matches were to be held in the nearby city of Barcelona, the capital of the Catalonia Region, and the richest city in Spain. The city boasted a long and prestigious footballing history.

Marco and Dani were sharing a double room. Granit had struck lucky, winning the draw for the only single room available for players. The coaching staff all had single rooms.

The *Brio Trio* were the only players selected from the French-speaking Romandie region of Switzerland. Not so surprising, given that seventy percent of the country's population are Swiss German. Dani and Granit had studied German at school for eight years, but their knowledge remained rudimentary. Marco's parents originated from the German-speaking part of the country before moving to Mézières, so he spoke his parents' Luzern Swiss-German dialect. At the training sessions, the coaches spoke mainly in high German, but also in French and, at times, in English. When they got angry, Swiss-German prevailed.

One of these training sessions had just ended, and the players had been given the afternoon off to explore the town and the beaches. On other national team tours in previous years, Granit had been inseparable from Dani and Marco. But this tour was different. Every time the team had been given time off, Granit had disappeared on his own, without telling anyone where he was going. That afternoon Dani and Marco decided to follow Granit from a distance to find out why.

The team returned to their hotel. Some stayed in their rooms playing video games; others headed towards town in small groups of twos and threes. Dani kept watch in the lobby and Marco from their balcony, which looked over the Sitges Mediterranean Sea promenade. Marco texted Dani to say he'd seen Granit heading south, on the beach.

They followed Granit from around a hundred meters away. After about one kilometer, Granit stopped and sat down on his towel looking around, as to see if anyone was watching. Dani and Marco kept their distance, using Dani's iPhone five camera to zoom in. On that part of the beach, there were only men, and many were swimming nude. Some strode together, hand-in-hand into the waves. At first, it didn't click. And then it did.

'He's on the gay beach, Marco,' Dani whispered. 'Do you think he's gay?'

'Does it matter?' Marco replied.

'No, it doesn't, not at all Marco. I've got many friends who are gay. He's our mate, always has been, and always will be. I don't care. Do you?'

'Of course not,' Marco replied. 'No worries. But how many openly gay professional footballers do you know?'

'Openly gay professional footballers? Good question. Not many.'

Marco continued. 'Well, that's the issue, Dani. It's not going to be easy for him to make it in football, is it? Many supporter groups are very homophobic.'

'It's not easy for others as well, Marco. What do you think it's like being half-African in our country, with some nutcase racists out there? OK for you, you're Swiss German. Whiter than whiter. Swisser than Swiss. Hey, let's get a little closer. This could be fun.' Dani giggled as he said it as if it were a kids' game.

'It's not funny, Dani. Let's leave him alone.' Marco was not joking.

Dani didn't reply and moved closer, using his camera to focus on Granit. And for fun, he said to Marco, he'd film Granit. What the hell. Just for a laugh.

Marco said that he wasn't going to have anything to do with this. He turned around and headed back up the beach towards the team hotel.

By the time Dani was within earshot, around ten meters away, another man, slighter older than Granit, had joined Granit and was sitting on the same towel. Suddenly, to Dani's surprise, the two began to kiss and embrace, before lying down on the sand together, hand in hand. Dani noticed a happy smile on Granit's face. An affectionate smile. A loving smile. The men seemed contented together.

Dani continued to film. No worries. He'd keep the footage for himself. He wasn't going to post it on Facebook, or anything stupid like that. Granit would never know he had it.

Ten meters away, as he was about to stop filming, Dani saw Granit staring at him, intently. He immediately turned around and started running back up the beach. He kept running for a full kilometre, not daring to look back to see whether Granit, who could run faster, was giving chase.

Granit remained on the beach, watching as Dani ran away, cowardly, into the distance. It wasn't worth the chase. Sure, he could beat the crap out of Dani if he wanted to. But what good would it do?

Granit also spotted Marco Zurcher further back in the distance, waiting for Dani. Marco, for God's sake! *Just proves you cannot even trust your closest friends.*

He started to slowly walk down the beach, in the opposite direction, pensively. As he walked, he reflected on where he was in life.

He was eighteen years old. Everybody told him he'd become one of the greatest football players of his generation, the GOAT, perhaps? If he played his cards right. On-going negotiations with Liverpool Football Club were progressing well. His agent, Dirk de Clippele, was truly fighting for him, securing him the best deal, dollar-by-dollar. Liverpool is where he *had* to be. Nowhere else. He'd visited the place earlier that year and loved it. The people were super friendly, the city had a vibrant nightlife, and Liverpool FC was a legend.

But why had his God tainted him so? Why was he born different? He hated it, but he loved it, at the same time. He was conflicted and had been that way since puberty. But as sure as he was born, Granit *knew* he must hide his sexuality *forever*. From everyone around him, not least his family.

There was no doubt in his mind that the professional football world - the clubs and the federations, the players and the managers, the owners, and the supporters - was *decades* away from accepting him and other gay players as they were. It just wasn't going to happen. No use pretending.

He vowed to himself that none of this would deter him. He was determined to make it. Now more than ever. He was stubborn. He'd do whatever it took.

Nothing would stop him. And he would stop at nothing. And to succeed, he must begin by saying goodbye to his old life.

Chapter Sixteen

*Two months later, in mid-September,
Dirk's house in Cologny, Geneva, Switzerland*

Granit never spoke to Dani and Marco again. Not on the training field and not during any games they played together for the national team from then onwards. Switzerland won the UEFA Under 18 European Football Championship in Spain, with Granit as the top goal scorer.

All the big European football leagues had sent scouts to the championship. Dirk de Clippele and Anita Patel had attended and had been busy signing new talent and finding buyers for their existing pool of young players. Thanks to Dirk's negotiating skills and Anita's legal expertise, both Granit and Dani had struck lucky. Dani was scooped up by English Premier League team Everton FC, and Granit by their city rivals Liverpool FC.

Both players moved to England and started their new careers in August of that year. After just six weeks in the first team at Liverpool, Granit became the youngest player to reach the ten-goal mark for the Reds. Dani, on the other hand, remained on the side-lines for the Blues of Everton, the team coach believing that he needed to beef up his body more to take the harder knocks of English Premier League football.

As for Marco Zurcher, Dirk had negotiated a sweet deal with the main sponsor of Lausanne Sports FC, a chemical company. Marco had the ability and the versatility to play in the German Bundesliga, or even in the English Premier League. But unlike most players with similar talent, Marco was a homeboy and wanted to remain loyal to his Academy team, to help it grow. Which it would, at a price that would keep Dirk in a steady income over many years to come. He'd even negotiated a clause that would keep him in the money if ever Marco was appointed coach of Lausanne Sports. Happy days.

It was late Saturday morning. Dirk and Anita were relaxing at one of Dirk's three houses. They were savouring brunch at the bottom of the garden of his lakeside house in Cologny, Geneva's most exclusive and richest neighbourhood.

One of Dirk's neighbours was a wealthy businessman from Kazakhstan, the other was a member of the Saudi Arabian royal family.

Not that he ever saw them unless they happened to be on their powerboats on the lake together.

Dirk's square-jawed and wide-shouldered chauffeur doubled up as both the house butler and their private pilot whenever Dirk and Anita flew, and they took to the skies a lot. They called him their *Batman*. This morning he was on butler duty and had served them their special Swiss breakfast of muesli, freshly baked croissants with devilled eggs and a Bucks Fizz for Anita. Dirk didn't drink alcohol, but Anita loved her champagne mixed with orange juice now and again What the hell: they had something to celebrate!

Dirk spoke first. 'Anita, one day, believe me, I'll marry you. You trust me, don't you?'

'I trust you like no one else in the whole wide world. More than my husband and kids. More than my parents, even. Patience, my dear. The timing is not right. You know the game. We make a great team in business and an even better couple in bed, *big man*. Guess you needed *extra time* this morning? That was so good. When's the replay?'

Dirk laughed. He adored Anita's provocative words about their bedroom exploits, every time. How she related them to football, his other passion. He loved it when they *sexted* on their mobiles, and he regularly sent Anita selfies of his genitals. He enjoyed being called the big man and always admired the sight of himself in the mirror after sex. Not one inch of fat on his sculptured, muscular body. Dirk took care of his body.

Yes, he would have made a great footballer, had he not had that terrible leg injury when he was seventeen years old. After the accident, his father had employed him at his abattoir business. Dirk could have taken it over and made a steady living when his dad retired, but his heart was in football. Always was. Always will be. And look at him now: the most successful football agent in Europe. In the world, perhaps. Beats chopping meat, any day of the week.

'Cheers, my dear!' Anita held up her Bucks Fizz to Dirk, who clinked it with his glass of freshly pressed, organic orange juice.

'Here's to our new signings. To our Swiss *Brio Trio*. And to a new contract every two years. Especially with Granit, don't you think?'

'He'll make us more money than all our other players combined. We need to be smarter. We need to adapt to the new world, Anita. How much did Neymar charge for the rights to his avatar in video games?'

'I dunno, *big man*. A lot, I guess?'

'Yes, more than you could imagine. I missed out on Neymar, as you will remember. But we're not going to miss out on Granit's avatar. No way. The metaverse is coming and we'll be earning much, much more from this than from shirts and other merchandising. Can you look into it please, *Pattie*?'

Dirk trusted just two people in the whole world: *Pattie* and his bodyguard. *Pattie* was Dirk's nickname for Anita.

'Sure. We've got to nurture his image. I'm worried about just one thing with Granit.'

'Injuries? So far, so good. He's a tough one.'

'It's not that, Dirk.'

'What is it, Pattie?'

'I can see that you don't have that sensitivity, that radar I've got.'

'Can you get to the point, please?'

While Dirk loved compliments, he got quickly irritated when he couldn't understand where the conversation was headed.

'He's gay, Dirk, had you not noticed?'

'Gay?'

'Sure. No problem with that in itself. I have many gay friends and so do you. Relatives as well. But tell me: how many professional footballers have come out of the closet, to your knowledge? Does *gay* and *accepted, successful footballer* go together? Sadly, not.'

Dirk was visibly shocked. Not about Granit being gay. Not at all. Dirk's elder brother was gay. Opposites in many ways, they had a bond that was stronger than most siblings.

Anita lit up a cigarette, a *Davidoff Slims*, inhaled it lovingly, and continued. 'If it ever gets into the media that Granit is gay, his career will be finished. And we can say goodbye to tens of millions of Euros in commissions and related earnings. No doubt about it. Football is not at all ready for this. How many of your players have ever come out? Women's *soccer* is more accepting, but the men's sport? It's going to take decades, *big man*.'

'Guess you're right, Pattie. I trust your judgment. We need to solve this for Granit. And for us. Give me a week, and I'll get back to you with a plan.'

'Can't wait. You'll find the right way around this issue. You always do, *big man*.'

At this point, Anita's phone vibrated. 'It's my husband. Must take it.'

Anita walked down the sloping, manicured lawn towards the lake. 'Hi, my sweetie. How are you? And the kids? Great hotel. Yes, the Hotel President. Wonderful view of the lake. Will send you pictures. I visited the school in the mountains yesterday. Yes. Of course. I've enrolled them for the next academic year. See you this evening. Can't wait as well. Love you too.'

Chapter Seventeen

FIVE YEARS AGO

Liverpool, England

After five years at the club, at just twenty-three years old, Granit was on track to become the GOAT – the **G**reatest **O**f **A**ll **T**ime scorer for Liverpool. All he had to do was to keep his present score rate up for a few more seasons and he'd surely beat the record. And at a younger age, to boot.

It was late March. Dirk and Anita had travelled together on their private jet to Liverpool to watch the match, the historic derby between the city rivals at Anfield, home of the Reds. Granit had invited them to stay at his recently finished, south-facing house overlooking the River Dee in Caldy on the Wirral. This is where many Liverpool footballers lived with their WAGs - their wives and girlfriends. Granit lived alone in his vast mansion. His life, his comings and goings, his property, and his car were protected by a handsome young hulk of a security guard who lived in a specially purposed guest house on the premises.

Dirk's two-year contract with Granit needed to be renewed, with revised clauses covering social media and merchandising. Granit Berisha made almost as much money on these deals as he did from his wages and transfer fee payments. Dirk de Clippele was also entitled to his cut. He did most of the representation and negotiation for Granit. Both parties were happy, and Granit had no intention of ditching Dirk for another agent. Why would he?

After years of searching, Anita Patel had finally found a video game company prepared to pay over ten million Euros for the exclusive right to use Granit's avatar. Dirk would pocket twenty percent of that amount, and Anita would make a five percent commission. Enough to pay the school fees for her teenage children at their prestigious boarding school in the beautiful mountain village of Villars-Sur-Ollon in Switzerland. Only the best for her kids. And as her husband had just lost his job at his hedge fund, she had figured she'd be wearing the pants for a while.

Dirk and Anita watched the game from the VIP lounge in the stadium. As Granit and his teammates came onto the pitch the crowd sang *You'll Never Walk Alone*, Liverpool's legendary anthem. The Everton supporters tried to sing theirs, *Spirit of the Blues*, but were quickly drowned out. Home advantage to Liverpool. And it stayed that way for the rest of the game, with Liverpool winning a tight and tense encounter one-zero. For once Granit was not on the score sheet.

After the game they had planned to meet for dinner with Granit at the Art School Restaurant, the best, and most expensive restaurant in town. Dirk and Anita arrived first and were shown to the downstairs aperitif lounge.

As their drinks were being served Dirk's phone vibrated.

'Dirk de Clippele, this is Dani Devaud on the line. How are you? I heard you were in town and wanted to catch up.'

'Dani, to what do I owe this pleasure?' To see the heavy frown on Dirk's face, the call was not a pleasure at all. Dirk was still Dani's agent, even if Dani was now playing in a lower league with northern English team Wigan Athletic. In Anita's words, Dani was a 'bread-and-butter' client. Steady income, all the same.

'We're about to have dinner with your old friend Granit.'

'Yes, I heard. Would there be space for me at the table, Dirk? Don't live too far away. I can get there in forty minutes. I haven't seen or spoken with Granit for years. Our ways parted and it's a real shame. You understand, Dirk, don't you?'

'I do Dani. I do. No problem. Let me see.'

Dirk did not want to have this conversation now. Nor did he want Dani at the dinner table. Then again, he didn't want to interfere in their friendship.

'Hang on Dani. I see that Granit is just arriving at the restaurant. I'll give him my phone and you can speak with him directly.'

Dirk handed Granit his mobile, saying that the caller wanted to speak to him, not mentioning Dani's name. Granit put his coat on the chair and took Dirk's mobile.

'Granit Berisha speaking. Who is this?'

Dani spoke in French. 'It's Dani, Granit. How are you, my old friend? About time we caught up, don't you think? I'm at Wigan Athletic now, not too far away. Let's fix something in our diaries. Would be nice to talk.'

Granit immediately blushed, angrily, as he heard Dani's voice. He excused himself to Dirk and Anita and stepped out of the restaurant onto an empty, rainy street for the remainder of the call.

'What do you want to talk about Dani? Do you want to blackmail me with that video you have of me back in Sitges? Do you want money? Wigan Athletic football club not paying you enough? I'm surprised you're still being selected for the national team, Dani. You were never that good.'

Dani was taken aback by Granit's aggression. He had forgotten about the time he'd filmed Granit kissing a man on the gay beach in Sitges. He wasn't even sure if he still possessed the old iPhone he used back then. And, for sure, the film would not be on the *cloud* as it wasn't standard at that time for iPhone fives. So, where's the problem, he wondered?

'Look, Granit, I just wanted to catch up. We've known each other since we were kids. I didn't realize…'

'You didn't realize I was gay until Sitges, Dani? Is it a big deal? No, it's not. And I think you agree. Not in the normal course of things of course. But we're professional footballers, Dani. How many fellow professional footballers do you know who are gay?'

Dani replied he knew quite a lot. Including some at his present club, Wigan. Granit continued, 'Fine. And how many of them have come out? Go on, tell me!'

Dani hesitated, 'You're right, Granit. Not many. I can't think of one top player who's come out, to be honest. You'd be the first.'

'Are you mad? No way. I've no intention of playing that role. I'm too big, and too famous to be known *the* gay footballer. No way. I have too much to lose. A lot of football fans are bigots when it comes to LGBT, even gay ones. Nobody wants to see a gay player in the red shirt at Liverpool. Sad, but true Dani. If I ever came out it would be the end of my career. I want to be remembered for my football, nothing else.'

'I get it, Granit, I do. Doesn't stop us from being friends.'

'We're never going to be friends again, Dani. You deceived me. Big time. Where is that video? I want you to destroy it And I want proof it's gone.'

'I don't know where it is, honestly Granit. I filmed you guys on an old phone. Probably threw it away.'

'Just get me that phone, Dani. You never throw things away. Just like your mother. *Mrs. Hoarder*, we used to call her. Bet she's still got those dish plates my dad stole from Balthazar's theatre for her.'

'Leave my mother out of this, Granit. There's no need to get personal. OK. I'll look. And if I find it, I'll give it to you. In person. Over dinner. And I'll pay for dinner, even though you're much richer than I am. Deal?'

'Call me when you find that phone. That's all I'm going to say. Get looking, now. Don't mess me around Dani. I have powerful friends who could harm you.'

'Is that a threat, my friend?'

Dani was beginning to wish he'd hadn't called Granit.

'It's a promise. Dani. You'll see. I can *destroy* you, don't forget.'

With that, Granit hung up and walked straight back into the restaurant, to the upstairs section, where Dirk and Anita were waiting for him at their table for dinner.

From Granit's angry and flustered appearance, Dirk and Anita guessed the call with Dani had not gone well. They moved the discussion on to the new deals that they'd been negotiating, and how to make the most of new media opportunities, in particular the use of Granit's avatar in video games.

Over the meal, Anita invited Granit to stay at Dirk's place in Geneva next week, reminding him they needed to officially sign off on the new two-year agent representation contract in the presence of a lawyer. Anita also explained they'd planned a surprise for him. A surprise that would change his life.

After the meal Granit's hulk of a chauffeur drove them all back to the house on the Wirrall. Anita and Dirk were given separate, magnificent guest suites, each with a balcony overlooking the River Dee and the scenic Welsh mountains on the far side. Beautiful.

Having been shown to his room by Granit's butler, Dirk immediately slipped over the landing to Anita's suite.

'What do you think Pattie? Are we on the right track? Do you think Granit will fall for our plan next week?'

'We'll see. Won't be easy for him. Firstly, *big man*, I want you to give me your phone.'

'Why? It is private.'

'I want to listen to the conversation between Granit and Dani. I know you record everything. I'm a lawyer, remember. A smart ass. Give me the phone.'

Dirk gave her the phone, reluctantly. Deep down he figured that Anita knew him better than he'd like to imagine.

Together they listened to the conversation on the speaker. They agreed that Dirk's plan for Granit was the best, given the circumstances. Quite frankly, Granit did not have much choice if he wanted to be remembered for his football, and not for his private life.

Business conversation over for the day, Anita glided slowly and invitingly into the bathroom and began to remove her make-up. Dirk followed her, putting his strong arms around her waist in a tight embrace, with his pelvis and erect penis pressing tightly against her curvaceous behind. He slowly moved his hand up her body and started to gently rub her breasts, staring at both her and his reflections in the gold-framed mirror. Life was good. And tonight, would be even better.

Chapter Eighteen

Three days later

Three days later it was Dirk and Anita's turn to host Granit, who had flown back to Switzerland for the international match weekend. Switzerland had to beat Norway at home to qualify for the UEFA European Championship. Granit Berisha would be heading up the Swiss attack. Marco Zurcher would be on the bench as a substitute. Dani had Devaud not been selected as he was still not fully fit from an early-season injury.

Entering Dirk's lakeside mansion in Coligny, Granit realized that he still had some way to go to match his agent's wealth. Dirk's place was worth five times Granit's house in England, if not more.

It was a beautiful, early Spring late morning, and the heat from the sun was warm enough to stage lunch in the trellis down by the lake. Dirk's butler had everything ready. No champagne this time; it was a working lunch.

Granit had expected the meeting to involve the signing of papers, new contracts and agreements with sponsors, and the like. But no. Just a friendly chit-chat and exchange of niceties. Very strange, Granit thought. Dirk and Anita never did *free lunches.*

Twenty minutes into the conversation, Anita looked up to the mansion from the trellis and shouted out 'Emina. How lovely of you to drop by. What an unexpected pleasure!'

She was referring to a most stunning woman who was being escorted over and down the lawn path by Dirk's butler to where they were now sitting in the trellis.

Granit turned around and saw this amazing creature. He somehow thought he recognized her. Had she been on the cover of a magazine he'd read recently? The connection made him think of his parents, now enjoying the high life back in Kosovo where he'd bought them a big house in their native village.

As Emina approached, keeping a strong visual lock on Granit and flirting as much as she could, Granit felt a twinge inside. Maybe he wasn't gay after all? Maybe he was bisexual?

'Granit, my dear. Allow me to introduce you to Emina. Otherwise known as *Miss Kosovo*. We've known each other for some time, haven't we Emina?'

Emina walked straight up to Granit who took her hand and feigned a kiss on the outside of her fingers. He'd seen this in some old movie and, on the spur of the moment, and considered it appropriate for the *beauty queen* of his parents' old country.

Emina responded, kissing Granit once on each cheek, and sat down beside him, her knee touching his.

'Seems you two are made for each other,' Anita said, somewhat prematurely.

Emina ignored her comment and immediately began talking to Granit in the Albanian language used by most Kosovans, the other being Serbian. Even though Granit had always spoken the language at home growing up with his parents, his Albanian was rusty. So, he let Emina do the talking, which suited him fine, being more the introvert and she the extrovert. It suited her as well.

Dirk and Anita left them to it and meandered back up the path to the house. They'd figured, correctly, that they'd have a couple of hours to kill before Emina and Granit were done. All was going perfectly to plan.

Chapter Nineteen

Three months later, Geneva City Hall Registry Office

Anita and Dirk's plan worked well. It took just three months for Granit and Emina to get married. They planned it as a small affair, with just a few key friends and witnesses, including Dirk and Anita, who took care of the organizational logistics.

In the presence of both the bride and the groom's parents, the civil wedding took place at the Geneva registry office. Both sets of parents had agreed to hold a religious ceremony and family get-together back in Kosovo in the summer, after the football season had ended.

Somehow the media got wind of it, and the international paparazzi were out in force to greet the happy couple as they arrived in different limousines at the registry office. Emina was looking ravishing in her *Gucci* outfit. The fashion house had clothed her from top to toe as part of a new modelling contract her agent had negotiated with the *House*. She'd be spending half of her time in Milan as a result, which nicely squared with her unwritten 'contract' with her husband-to-be. For his attire, Granit decided to be dressed exclusively by *Tom Ford*, with which he'd had a sponsoring contract for the past two years.

What a great looking couple! What beautiful, perfect people!

Granit had been told many times by the girls he looked like a twenty-five-year-old George Clooney, though he didn't see the resemblance himself when he looked in the mirror. Off the football field, he still lacked self-confidence.

The marriage ceremony was followed by a small reception at Dirk's place in Cologny. It took place on the same lawn where the couple had met, just three months previously, gently sloping down to the shores of Lake Geneva, with its private jetty. And it was from there that Granit and Emina departed in a high-powered speed boat headed for a luxurious yacht anchored further up the lake on the French side, near the beautiful medieval town of Yvoire. The get-away was so meticulously planned, not that even the paparazzi got to spoil their first evening as husband and wife, Mr. and Mrs. Berisha, the hottest couple in the English Premier League. Their honeymoon was to be short: just one night on the boat before they both headed off for their respective professional duties.

Before going to bed that night, Emina texted her elder sister, who had remained in Kosovo. *Tied the knot today. So happy to have found my perfect match. Such a gentleman. The arrangement suits us well. See you in Milan next week. Bring your new man, Kuijtim. And you'll meet Luigi. Can't wait.*

Chapter Twenty

Granit and Emina's house in Caldy, Wirral, near Liverpool, England

Two days later Granit returned to England and Emina flew back from Milan that morning, private jet.

Today they were to be interviewed by Sanjay Singh, the editor of the *Liverpool Post*. The gig had been organized by Dirk, who wouldn't be present this time. He'd decided to entrust Granit's media relations activities to Emina, whose great looks and Miss Kosovo body conveniently disguised a very smart intellect and quick-witted brain.

Sanjay Singh was escorted by Granit's young hulk of a security guard into the salon. Wow! This room along is bigger than my whole apartment downtown, Sanjay thought. And what a view! Those must be the Welsh mountains on the other side of the river.

Granit entered the room with Emina on his arm, designer clothes oozing *Tom Ford* and the *House of Gucci*. Sanjay stood up to greet them.

'Sit down, Mr. Singh, please.' Emina took the lead from the start. Wearing the pants.

'Welcome to our humble abode.' *Such great English language skills* thought Sanjay. She's even used that most upper-class expression, *humble abode*. The woman will go far.

'Tea?'

Sanjay would have preferred a single malt but knew better.

'Many thanks. Darjeeling, if you have it?'

'Of course.' Emina sent the security guard to prepare the tea.

'Mr. Singh. We thought we'd get the sports editor for our interview, not you in person, the prestigious editor-in-chief. We are extremely flattered and honoured to welcome you today.'

'Many thanks, Mrs. Berisha. The pleasure is mine. Any problem if I record this conversation with my phone?'

'No problem at all. In any case, I know you will send me a copy of the article prior to publication,' Emina replied, insistently.

Sanjay never did this. But there was something about the magnetism of this woman that made him oblige. He confirmed to Emina he'd send the article that evening. It was due for publication the next day, so he'd appreciate a quick reply from Emina. No problem, she knew what she was doing.

They spent the next two hours discussing, with Sanjay asking the questions and Emina doing most of the answering. The article was published the next day.

Chapter Twenty-One

English Football Premier League hottest couple share intimacy with Post readers

Exclusive interview with Granit and Emina Berisha

Sanjay Singh, Editor-in-chief, Liverpool Post

Initially, I was going to send Jack, my rookie sports editor. But this interview required a little more media experience. Selfishness took over, and I found myself in the 'front room' if you could call it that, of the biggest house in Caldy.

Trying hard to ignore the breath-taking view over the River Dee to the Welsh mountains beyond, I stroll into the living room of the newly wed, glamourous couple's palatial house and shake hands with Granit and Emina Berisha.

Emina gives me a couple of cheeky pecks on my cheeks, making me blush as her piercing green eyes meet mine. I remain suitably calm and controlled.

Yes, I guess you could say that their lounge was bigger than my whole house. And the balcony than my kitchen. So what? Does it matter? The man deserves it. After just a handful of seasons at the club, Granit Berisha is about to become the leading goal-scorer for Liverpool FC.

It's Emina's idea to give their first interview as a married couple to the Liverpool Post. She says she's quickly become attached to our great city and wants to connect more with its people.

Emina was elected Miss Kosovo four years ago when she was just eighteen. Most of our readers already know that. She then took a degree in Communications and Fashion at the University of Milan, where she graduated with first-class honours. Smart cookie. She now models with the House of Gucci in Milan and has created her own agency, appropriately named **FE***mina Communications.*

Both Granit and Emina come from humble backgrounds. Granit's parents moved from their native Kosovo to a country village near Lausanne in Switzerland in the 1990s. His mother cleaned houses and his father washed dishes in the local café kitchen and was a handyman at the local village theatre. They lived in a tiny apartment above the theatre costume depot, provided by the theatre owner as part of their remuneration. Together his parents made just enough to cover the bills and finance their annual trip back home to Kosovo, borrowing a friend's car for the trip.

From the age of eight, each Granit walked three miles every evening after school to the local football ground, where he finetuned his skills. He preferred to play with the older kids, staying on past dark. His parents never seemed to worry about where he was, or what he was up to.

Money was always tight. As he continues his life story, Granit's eyes water, especially when he talks about the sacrifices his parents made to ensure he had the right kit, bag, boots, and clothes, so as not to feel in any way different from his richer friends.

But different, he felt. And different, he tells me, is how he still feels today.

He played for the Academy at Lausanne Sports FC as a teenager and felt good there. He reminisces about watching their senior team from a stand called the 'Kop Sud'. He was part of a supporter group called Loz Boys. Little did he ever realize he'd end up playing in front of the real, genuine thing, he tells me enthusiastically, the one and only Liverpool Kop with the crowd chanting 'You'll Never Walk Alone' as the team comes on to the hallowed turf, and at the end of each game, win or lose. What loyalty and adoration! No other supporters come close; Granit tells me. I don't tell him I'm an Everton supporter.

Liverpool is the best place for a quiet guy like him, he repeats to me for the third time. When I ask 'why', he tells me he prefers others to do the talking. He's in the right city, I reply. Scousers love to talk.

Emina takes the lead, once again, taking up the slack. Would I like to know the significance of Granit's trademark hand movements each time he scores a goal? Sure, I say. After each goal, whichever stadium he's in, Granit looks in the direction of Kosovo, where his parents now live in a mansion, he had built for them in their home village. He firstly puts both hands on his chest, then extends them outwards, reaching upwards. He then makes a full ball-like circle sign with his hands

Granit turns shy and blushes as Emina explains. The hands placed on his chest relate to him. The hands reaching out represent his parents. And the circle means that the family is together and always will be.

Tears reach my eyes. I almost cry. How beautiful!

Emina suddenly becomes all excited, momentarily losing her composure. She stands up and tells me excitedly that Granit will be adding something new to his signature goal gesture next time he scores. I was curious. What could that be?

Emina says I'll find out on Saturday when he scores next. I push for more. Ok, she says. Let me tell you. I'm pregnant.

Wow, I reply. Girl or boy?

You'll find out.

I congratulate them profusely. We talk a little longer, then say warm goodbyes. I'd be welcome anytime at the VIP lounge, Emina whispers to me as I get into my car and wave goodbye to England's most beautiful and elegant football couple.

PART THREE

THE PRESENT TIME

Chapter Twenty-Two

Tuesday morning, December 29

Marianne had hardly slept a wink. It was five in the morning; she was already awake and buzzing. Time to get to the office. Early, again. She was beginning to make a habit of this.

Yesterday, before she left Police HQ, DI Favre had told her that the message she'd found on the deceased Balthazar's iPhone was now a *line of inquiry*. More research was needed.

What did old Balthazar mean when he asked that question to Kevin? And why would he record that conversation? And did Kevin know he was being recorded?

Tell me the truth now Kevin, Balthazar had said. *Was it Marco and Dani in that ambulance last night? Was it their dead bodies bumping around in the back? Did you kill them, Kevin? What did you do with their bodies?*

Favre had also instructed Marianne to dig deeper. The first question was *motive*. Once they'd found that, they'd bring Kevin in for questioning. Better to have all the ducks in a row before proceeding, Favre insisted.

Why would Kevin want to kill Marco and Dani? Marianne had known Kevin since she was five years old when she used to hang out with her brother and the bigger boys at the football ground at FC Jorat Mézières. Granit, Marco, and Dani formed the *Brio Trio*. Kevin was a good player, but never fully fitted in. He was never part of the gang. He tagged along. He wanted to be the *fourth musketeer*, but he was never fully accepted. Why?

Then she remembered. That rumour. Of course. Her brother Dani had told her once, but she'd thought it was just village gossip. Kevin's father was the illegitimate son of a brother and a sister? Really? In this day and age?

Was being teased about this motive enough to kill someone? Could that be why Kevin wanted Dani dead? A long shot, Marianne thought. Then again, she was beginning to learn that literally *anyone* could be a suspect in a murder case. This was police work; she needed to become more suspicious, by nature.

76

She entered the police headquarters just after six in the morning, expecting to be the first at her desk; DI Favre was already there, in his glass office.

'Morning boss. Regarding our suspect, Kevin Gillicion I think I've found a clear reason for him to be angry.' Marianne didn't believe the incest story was strong enough to provide motive for murder, but she figured she'd test it on Favre all the same

'Fire away, Miss early bird.'

'Incest, boss. Rumour has it that Kevin's dad's parents were siblings. I remember my brother Dani telling me about this. He was a bit of a jerk with Kevin and took the piss out of him about it. They once came to blows about it.'

'Good work, Marianne. I've seen people murdered for much less. *Motive* is a fascinating area of research. You need to get some of that into your doctoral thesis. Maybe this case will give you some good data What are the three biggest motives for murder, Marianne?'

Marianne scratched her head. She remembered reading this on the internet.

'Lust, love, loathing, and loot. The four Ls, boss.'

'Very good.' Favre could sound so patronizing at times.

'And Kevin, in this context?'

'Loathing.

'Talk me through your reasoning, Marianne.'

'OK, here goes. Kevin wanted to be liked and admired by his three best mates when he was a kid - Granit, Dani and Marco. They were all good footballers, and so was Kevin. But he was never let into the *Brio Trio* gang. Instead, one of them, Dani – my brother – pushed him away, taunting him about the rumour of incest in his family. Little by little Kevin started to loathe my brother and, to a lesser extent, Granit, and Marco.'

'So far, so good Marianne. Keep going.'

'They grow apart. The *Brio Trio* become highly paid professional footballers. Kevin, on the other hand, follows an apprenticeship and becomes a municipal employee in Servion. This job gives him access to many interesting places around the village, including spots where dead bodies could be hidden.'

'For example?' interrupted Favre

77

'The municipal trash tip. The village graveyard. The school and the chapel. He also has keys to the theatre from Balthazar as well as to the zoo, as he is one of the qualified marksmen to stun the animals should there be a fire at the place.'

'What?'

'Sure, boss. The volunteer fire department in Servion has specially trained people who keep a tranquilizer gun in their homes in case animals escape from the zoo. They pick them from the best shots at the *Abbaye*.'

For a moment Philippe Favre had no idea what Marianne was talking about. Then he remembered. The *Abbaye* was an annual rifle shooting competition that takes place in many villages in Vaud Canton.

Marianne continued. 'Kevin is the President of the Servion-Ferlens-Essertes *Abbaye*. A top shot, I've heard.'

'I'll remember that when we get around to arresting him,' ironized Favre. 'You're not finished. We've got a motive, *loathing*. We now need to figure out *how* he killed your brother and Marco, if he did, which we don't yet know. For the moment they are just missing persons, of course.'

Marianne felt like she was in a surreal movie. Here she was, theorizing intellectually about a possible real murder, and the victim could be her brother. One minute she felt like breaking down in tears. The next, her rational brain was juggling with potential murder scenarios.

She continued. 'Let's dissect the recording on Balthazar's phone. *Was it Marco and Dani in that ambulance last night? Was it their dead bodies bumping around in the back?* That's what he said. We need to know what ambulance? What were they doing in that ambulance? And where were they going?'

'My fault, Marianne, I should have told you.'

Philippe realized he'd not yet given Marianne the information Fabienne Pasche had related to him the other night when he visited her.

'I learned from the Servion Syndique the other evening that she'd seen Kevin at the wheel of what appeared to be the same mock ambulance that was used on stage during the show. There were two other people in the car, but they had masks on, so the Syndique could not identify them. Now I'm guessing that one of those people was Balthazar. We need to identify the other person in the car.'

'I'm sure Kevin will spill the beans when we question him.'

'Don't' be so sure, young lady.' Favre was patronizing her again.

He continued; poker faced. 'We're not allowed to torture our suspects, though sometimes I wish we were,'

Marianne thought she'd got it. He *was* joking, right?

'Of course, boss, ha-ha. How do we explain the masks?'

'You haven't heard about the secret solstice sect of Servion, Marianne?' Philippe was certainly taking the piss now. Marianne decided to play dumb. 'No. Please tell me, dear boss.'

Favre gave Marianne a quick summary of what Fabienne had told him about the tradition of the solstice sect.

Marianne continued. 'We now have four, maybe five, even six places Kevin could have hidden the bodies. The theatre. The chapel on the hill. The cemetery. The menhir.'

'And the two *maybe* places?'

'The sewage works, which is on the road to the cemetery. We call it the STEP. And the zoo. Let's not forget. Kevin has a key.'

'And the trash tip makes seven, and the school, eight.'

'Forgot about them. Where do we start?'

Favre didn't reply for a while.

'How well do you know Kevin?'

'Pretty well.'

'Did you ever have a relationship with him?'

Marianne was shocked and blushed. How did Favre know that? It was a good six or seven years ago and only lasted for a few weeks.

'Yes, for a very short time. And it wasn't love. He's a nice guy, but I've outgrown the village and he's still there. He'll always be a simple village boy.'

'When I bring him in for questioning, I want you to watch and listen from the observation room upstairs. Don't worry, he won't know you're there.'

Fascinated by Favre's story of the solstice sect, Marianne spent her lunchtime searching the internet for more information. After twenty minutes she clicked on a link to an abstract from a Lausanne University Bachelor thesis by a History Department student entitled *The Servion Solstice Sect: A Two-Thousand-Year-Old Tradition?*

It was written thirty-five years ago. The author was a certain David Gillieron. Kevin's father, perhaps? And why the question mark?

Chapter Twenty-Three

The same day, Servion village cemetery

Kevin Gillieron loved his job at the Servion Municipality. Of course, he'd have preferred to be a professional footballer, like his childhood mates Granit, Dani, and Marco. Having left school at the age of sixteen, he'd done his apprenticeship with the municipality. When the previous municipal employee retired after forty years, Kevin felt truly privileged to take over. It was a job for life. He now had his own apprentice, who was as keen to learn the ropes as he'd been.

The best thing about his job was the variety. In the morning he could be managing the comings and goings at the municipal dump, ensuring the recycling was done correctly and the place was kept spick and span. In the afternoon he could be planting trees along the roadside as part of the municipality's carbon-neutral efforts. And the next day he'd be repairing fixtures for the kids at the school playground.

Today he was at the village cemetery, a place he knew well. In addition to Balthazar, there had been a couple of other deaths in the village those past few days. Kevin was preparing two graves for burials later in the week. It was arduous work, especially in winter. He and his apprentice took turns in digging out the clay-heavy soil, down to the recommended depth of two metres.

Balthazar's body had been taken away for an autopsy and had not yet been released. In such cases, it could be weeks before the authorities released the body. Forever the control freak, Balthazar had made his *afterlife* wishes well known to Kevin on several occasions. He'd written clear instructions. Yes, he wanted to be buried in the family plot. And yes, he wanted people to mourn, wail and cry. And yes, most importantly, it *must* be on that *special day*.

Balthazar had instructed Kevin to organize his burial at the mid-point between the solstice and the equinox. This meant waiting for another month, until February 2nd. Could they keep him in cold storage until then? What was so special about that day?

Each time Kevin worked in the cemetery he was reminded of his past. Specifically, that horrible rumour that had probably pushed his dad to commit suicide. Where had his grandparents - the supposed siblings -

been buried? Not here, that's for sure? No trace in the Servion graveyard. Nobody seemed to know. Rumour had it they'd been buried down by the menhir. If so, why?

Each headstone in the cemetery told its own life and death story. Both of Kevin's parents were buried a patch at the bottom corner. His mother had died when he was two. Breast cancer. He didn't have any conscious memories of her. He recognized most of the names on the other headstones. Many were relatives, and the ones that weren't were friends, or friends of friends. Small village. There was not one headstone name he did not recognize.

Thinking about family, he wondered if he'd ever find a woman who'd want to create a family with him. He'd really liked Marianne. She was fun, and they got along well. Had a good laugh together. But it hadn't lasted long. He'd never felt good enough for her. Not smart enough. Too local. She'd never actually called him a *paywai*– a derogatory term for country boy – but Kevin had felt she'd wanted to, at times. He knew he was quite handsome, attractive to women, because he regularly got top hits on Tinder. Apart from sex, nothing serious had developed from them.

The cemetery looked out over wide, rich arable fields sloping down the long hill towards the *Broye* river valley and the market town of Oron-la-Ville, over and back up the incline to the famous town of Gruyères, where the cheese of the same name was created nine-hundred years ago. The whole valley view was a magnificent, uninterrupted vista.

Bearing down on the fortified old medieval town was the Moléson, a wide, majestic mountain in the Fribourg canton pre-alps region. Snow covered the top of the Moléson, as Kevin looked. Local folklore warned farmers not to plant until the snow had melted at least twice on that the Moléson, otherwise, the crops would fail.

Kevin was discussing this with his apprentice when his phone started vibrating.

'Gillieron,' Kevin answered.

'Police. Mr. Gillieron?'

'Yes- What can I do for you?'

'Sorry to bother you. We need you to come down to the station for questioning. Immediately.'

'Why?'

81

'We will tell once you arrive. Please report to our HQ at Blécherette, as soon as possible.'

Kevin asked whether this had anything to do with Balthazar's death?

'We cannot say anymore now, sir.'

Chapter Twenty-Four

The same day, Blécherette Police HQ

Kevin arrived at Police HQ at one p.m. that afternoon and was escorted to the interview room. Marianne took her place at the observation window. She looked down to the table below where DI Favre was seated, with Kevin opposite. It felt unreal. Kevin looked straight at her a few times, and she looked away and blushed. Then she came back to her senses. He could not see her. Stupid. Such a weird sensation.

Favre explained to Kevin that he was in this room voluntarily to answer questions and to help with police inquiries. Favre reassured Kevin he had not been arrested. Kevin appeared calm and relaxed.

'Before we start, can you please confirm your name,' Favre said, kicking off the interview.

'Gillieron, Kevin.'

'Thank you. Can I call you Kevin?'

'Sure, can I call you Philippe?' Kevin replied, nonchalantly.

In her observation booth, Marianne sneered to herself. Poor *paywai*, the derogatory slang word for country folk in Vaud canton. When was the last time you got out of your little village of Servion? This is not a joke, Kevin. If you've had anything to do with my brother's death, we'll find out. Trust me. Don't be a *paywai!*

Favre decided to be more formal and spoke directly.

'Monsieur Gillieron, we have reason to believe you are aware of the whereabouts of two missing persons.'

'Missing persons? Who?'

'When was the last time you saw Dani Devaud and Marco Zurcher?'

'Are they missing?'

'Would you like me to repeat the question Monsieur?'

'I really can't remember. I know they were at the theatre the other night, dressed up as Santas. But I was behind the curtains, so I couldn't see them. In any case, how would I have recognized them, if they were dressed up as Santas?'

'I'm asking the questions, not you.'

'I've not spoken to either of them for a long time. I'm not important to them, you see. I'm a nobody to them.'

'What do you mean by that, Monsieur Gillieron?'

'We were friends when we were kids. And I dated Dani's sister Marianne some years ago. But that's it. They're much too far above my station, aren't they?'

'In what way?'

'You know the reply to that question, detective. They're international football stars. I'm just a humble jack-of-all-trades employee at the Servion municipality. Why would they want to spend any time with me?'

'Monsieur Gillieron. I repeat my question. When was the last time you saw Dani Devaud and Marco Zurcher?'

'I've answered that question. You say I'm here voluntarily. Ok then. I've had enough. Can I go now?'

'Just wait here. I'll be back in a minute.'

Favre realized that he'd gotten off to a bad start. He left the room and went straight upstairs to speak to Marianne.

'Marianne, is he lying?'

Marianne was surprised that Favre had come up to her so soon for her opinion. They'd only started the interview a few minutes ago.

'No. Not at all. He's just trying to be nonchalant, boss. He's always thought of himself as a bit of a smart ass. But his jokes? Fine at the local *Abbaye,* or village fête. Not when you're with your university friends debating Carl Jung over dinner.'

'Hmm. So, he's been telling the truth so far?'

'In my opinion, yes.' Favre didn't reply. He went straight back down to the interview room.

Kevin asked Favre again if he could leave, as he had to get back to work.

'You can leave whenever you want, Monsieur Gillieron. Your boss, Madame Pasche knows you're here. No need to worry about missing work. She told me it would be ok. She told me that you'd be very willing to help us with our inquiries. That you were an exemplary employee.'

These words made Kevin feel better. More supported. Favre was spinning a yarn, something he did occasionally. He felt ok doing this if it helped get to the truth and, especially, to a confession. He'd call Fabienne Pasche later to brief her.

Kevin said he'd stay, but he needed to be back for the opening of the trash tip at five p.m. that afternoon.

Three hours remaining, thought Favre. Three hours to get closer to the truth. He knew Kevin was hiding something but couldn't pinpoint it. It would take time and different angles of attack.

'Monsieur Gillieron. At the FC Jorat fundraising event at the theatre the other night, what were your tasks?'

'Balthazar had me on the stage curtain that night. I also had to drive the ambulance on and off the stage. It was for the scene when old *Weymo* broke his leg. I was there when it happened. I was there with my dad. That was before…'

'Before what, Kevin?' Favre guessed Kevin was thinking about his father's death.

'Before nothing.'

Favre wasn't sure if bringing up the subject of his dad's suicide would help, so he moved the conversation on.

'What did you think happened that night at the theatre? Why did all the lights go out? And why did the fire alarm go off?'

'Because he told me to do it.'

'Who told you to do what?'

'Balthazar. It was written on the stage instructions we all received for the evening. CUT ELECTRICITY AND SOUND FIRE ALARM at the entr'acte when the two Santas fall over on stage. That was what I was instructed to do. It was weird, but I assumed it was all part of the act.'

'Didn't you think to check this with Balthazar beforehand?'

'He was busy. I was just following instructions. *His* instructions.'

'Kevin, are you telling the truth?'

'Yes. Sure I am. Why would I lie?'

'OK, thanks very much for your time. You've been very helpful. You're free to go. We will want you in again for further questions. We'll give you a call when.'

'That's it, then?'

'Yes, thanks. Safe trip back to Servion.'

Marianne had watched the whole time from the observation room. She was confused. She had not understood what her boss was trying to do. Back in his office, she was ready to fire.

'Boss, I'm not trying to be smart but why did you let him go so easily? Why didn't you confront him with the tape we have from Balthazar asking him if he killed Dani and Marco?'

'Too soon,' Favre replied. 'This is a complicated case. If it turns out Kevin did murder Dani and Marco – and let's not forget, we haven't found any bodies yet – we'll need to slowly coerce him into a confession.'

'Do *you* think it's him, boss?'

'I think he's hiding something.'

'What do we do now?'

'We bring him in again tomorrow for more questioning. Meantime, I'll call the Servion Syndique to brief her. She's on our side.'

Marianne had a thought.

'Boss. For tomorrow's interview, let's make things simpler If I think he's lying, I'll ping you a message on your mobile. No text, just a sad *emoji* face.'

'Good idea. Thanks for proposing it.'

Marianne was once again pleased with herself. Favre was beginning to accept her.

Chapter Twenty-Five

The next day, Blécherette, Police HQ Interview Room

First thing the next morning, Kevin went straight to the Syndique's office located in the old village school, just up the road from the theatre. He trusted his Syndique, even though she'd often had issues with Balthazar.

During their discussion, Fabienne Pasche advised him to cooperate fully with the police inquiry. She reassured him that everything would be fine. That he was *not* a suspect. That he had nothing to worry about. She was lying, of course.

The same policewoman who called Kevin yesterday called again, asking him to get to Police HQ for two p.m. that afternoon. Same place. Same interview room. Same DI Favre.

Kevin was there on time.

Favre kicked off the proceedings, with Marianne once again watching, invisibly, from the observation room.

'Thanks once again for coming in. Madame la Syndique informed me that all will be good at work, so no need to worry on that front.'

'Thanks, detective. I still don't know why I'm here?'

'Let's continue from yesterday. You confirmed you cut off the electricity mains in the theatre, then hit the fire alarm. Correct?'

'Yes. I was merely following the instructions all the stagehands received.'

'Well, that's the rub, Kevin. We've checked with the other stagehands. One of them gave us a copy of the instructions she'd received from Balthazar. No mention of cutting the electricity or sounding the fire alarm.'

'If you don't believe me, I can give you the sheet I received with the instructions. I've got it at home.'

'Thanks. We'll certainly follow that up. You also said yesterday that you drove the mock ambulance on and off the stage. Correct?'

'Yes.'

'When you drove this vehicle off the stage it was dark. Because you'd cut the electricity.'

'That's right. Just following instructions. I know the theatre like the back of my hand. It was easy. Didn't even have to use the headlights. Drove it straight out, backstage, and out onto the parking lot as instructed.'

'Did you notice anything moving in the back of the ambulance?'

'No. Not at all. It was all so quick. I was done in three minutes. I left the ambulance outside, plugged the electricity line into the socket at the back, locked it, and came back into the theatre.'

'You connected the ambulance to the electricity? Why?'

'That's what I was told to do by Balthazar. We use that same ambulance to transport food from our caterer in Oron. There was some frozen food still in the back and we needed to refrigerate the truck to minus sixteen Celsius,'

'How did you know there was food in the back? Did you open it up?'

'No, I didn't. Everyone knew. The ambulance was an expensive gift from that football agent to the theatre. It doubled up as a frozen delivery van. Uncle B was well-pleased when he was given that.'

'Uncle B?'

'Balthazar. He's not my uncle really, he's my second cousin. He helped me when my dad…'

Kevin suddenly dried up. Once again, Favre decided not to follow this line of inquiry. Not yet.

'Monsieur Gillieron. Kevin. You say that you didn't hear any movement in the back of the ambulance. How do you explain this?'

Favre decided it was time to get tough. He played Kevin the recording from Balthazar's phone.

Tell me the truth now Kevin. Was it Marco and Dani in that ambulance last night? Was it their dead bodies bumping around in the back? Did you kill them, Kevin? What did you do with their bodies?

Kevin put his head into both hands and slumped, with his head resting on the interview table. Favre said nothing. He wasn't sure whether Kevin was crying, or just holding back the tears.

Marianne looked on from the observation room and felt a bit sorry for Kevin. He lived on his own. Both his parents were dead. He didn't have many friends.

After a few minutes of silence, Favre spoke up.

'Can you please confirm this is the voice of Balthazar, Kevin? Or Uncle B, as you called him?'

'Yes, of course, it is.'

'So why would he say what he said? Were the bodies of Dani Devaud and Marco Zurcher in the back of the ambulance you were driving that night?'

'I wasn't driving that ambulance that night. As I said, all I did was drive it on and off the stage and park it up.'

Out of nowhere, Favre's phone pinged. A sad face *emoji* appeared. It was from Marianne. Kevin was lying.

Favre had figured this out for himself. He knew from Fabienne Pasche that Kevin had been at the wheel of that same mock ambulance on his way to the cemetery, at one a.m. Favre had also deduced that Balthazar was one of the two others in the front seats. And that this was the trip he was referring to in the recording on his phone.

'Monsieur Gillieron, I don't believe you.'

'Honest, it's the truth, detective.'

'Ok. We have a reliable witness who told us she saw you driving the mock ambulance on your way to the cemetery at around one o'clock in the morning. We have reason to believe your Uncle B was also in the car as well as a so-far unidentified third person. He and Balthazar were wearing the traditional masks used for the solstice worship. No need to deny it, Kevin. We know about the whole thing'

'It's not true. All lies. That never happened.'

Favre's phone pinged again, with another sad face emoji and a short message from Marianne. *Let me speak with Kevin, please.*

Chapter Twenty-Six

That same afternoon, the office of Madame la Syndique, Servion

Fabienne Pasche, the Servion Syndique, had two offices. One at the communal building in Les Cullayes, a neighbouring village that merged with Servion a few years ago, and the other one where she was today, in the old schoolhouse in Servion village. Her office was on the second floor, overlooking a playground for smaller kids and some public toilets, where older kids would hang out and smoke weed. Most of the weed they smoked was grown and supplied by the local farmers.

After Philippe Favre's briefing the previous day, Fabienne Pasche had decided to do a little investigative work herself. She'd summoned Kevin's apprentice into her office for some questions. He was there now.

Fabienne could not remember his name, offhand. The fresh-faced apprentice looked no more than twelve years old, thought Fabienne, as he entered her office, timidly. Had she not been his employer, she'd have sent a note to the social services asking them to check on his eating habits, he was so skinny. Still, his rosy cheeks suggested the outdoor life suited him.

'Enjoying your apprenticeship, young man?'

'Love it, Madame la Syndique. And thank you once again for selecting me. I appreciate it very much, and so do my parents. They are really grateful.' Not all youngsters are impolite, Fabienne reflected.

'All good with your boss, Kevin Gillieron?'

'Yes, very good. I'm learning a lot from him.'

'Good. I just need to ask you a few questions. Nothing serious. Just part of the evaluation we do for our apprentices. We want to make sure that you are being treated right.'

'Sure. Happy to help.'

Fabienne wondered where to start. The cemetery. Why not?

'I see you've been digging some graves in the cemetery.'

'Hard work, that is. We've got two burials later in the week.'

'And any other graves being dug?'

'Yes, but I'm not supposed to know.'

Fabienne was immediately intrigued. 'Where, exactly?'

'I think it's for his Uncle B, as he calls him. There's a family plot and Kevin's been working on it after hours. He's covered the area with a tarpaulin and told me not to go there.'

'I see. Anything else you'd like to tell us? Anything else out of the ordinary?'

'We went over to the menhir yesterday. Kevin told me that this was not our responsibility.'

'Why did you go, then?'

'Kevin said he just wanted to check things out. He spent some time prodding around on each side of the river with a big, pointed metal bar. As if he were looking for avalanche victims in the snow.'

'Did he find anything?'

'Don't think so. And then we headed off to the STEP – you know, the local sewage works. Hate it there. The smell…'

'I can understand. What did you do there?'

'Same thing. Kevin was prodding around again with those pointed metal bars into two of the sewage vats. We were only there for a few minutes, then we went to the dump.'

'Anything out of the ordinary at the dump?'

'Not really. He started a fire at the back, where people leave their tree branches and leaves. I was surprised. I learned in my apprenticeship studies that we should not use petrol anymore to light the fire. Maybe Kevin never learned that?'

'Did he use petrol?'

'Yeah, litres of the stuff. That fire must have been burning all night.'

Fabienne's brain was working overtime. Between the cemetery, the menhir, the sewage works, and the dump there seemed to be some weird stuff happening.

'Thank you very much for your time.' Fabienne showed the boy out. Well, he was sixteen. Is that still a boy, she thought? Yes, and no.

Picking up her phone, she called Philippe Favre.

Chapter Twenty-Seven

Later that afternoon, Blécherette Police HQ, Interview Room

Philippe Favre looked again at Marianne's text. He saw the sad face *emoji*, indicating that Kevin was lying about driving the ambulance to the cemetery. And her request for her to talk with Kevin directly? Why not? What did he have to lose? He texted back. *Meet me outside the interview room, now.*

Marianne rushed down.

'I'm ok with this, Marianne. But not on your own. I'm going to be there with you.'

'No problem,' Marianne replied. 'Please let me do the talking. I think I can get him to open up, to tell us his whole story. At present he's frightened. He's probably been sworn to secrecy about all that solstice nonsense. He's not the sharpest tool in the shed.'

'Let's go! After you.'

As Marianne entered the room Kevin got up and walked over to greet her, which meant three kisses on the cheeks in Vaud Canton protocol. Marianne immediately backed off.

'No kisses. Kevin, please sit down. I'm here in an official capacity.'

'Good to see you too, Marianne. Hope you're keeping well. Heard that you're some sort of big fish at the University of Lausanne Criminology department. Didn't realize you'd become a cop.'

'I haven't, Kevin. Like you, I'm just helping DI Favre with his investigation. Dani's gone missing, for God's sake. Don't you understand? My brother. Something deep down tells me he is dead, Kevin, dead.'

'I'm sorry about that,' Kevin replied, 'but I have nothing to do with that.'

Favre butted in. 'Monsieur Gillieron, Marianne Devaud is *not* officially part of this investigation team. However, I strongly urge you to listen to her and to take her advice. She has been giving us some important information and will continue to do so.'

'Thank you, Detective Inspector Favre. May I continue?'

Favre nodded.

'Kevin, we need to know the truth, the full truth. What were you doing that night? I know about the solstice stuff. We all do. All the village, and beyond. I know you've been sworn to secrecy, but Balthazar is dead now. He won't tell. Who was the other person in the ambulance that night?'

Kevin muttered to himself.

'Sorry,' Marianne said, 'I didn't get that?'

'Graff,' Kevin replied.

'Would that be Yves Graff?'

'Could be.'

Marianne took DI Favre aside and explained.

'Boss it appears that the third person in the mock ambulance that night was Mr. Yves Graff, the farmer who lives across the road from the chapel on the hill in Servion. Like Balthazar, he's a second cousin to Kevin.'

On receiving this information, Favre left the interview room, phone in hand. Marianne guessed he was sending someone to interview Mr. Graff, immediately.

Marianne sat back down at the interview table with Kevin. Favre had sent in a uniformed policeman to keep an eye on proceedings and for Marianne's protection.

While Favre was out, Kevin slipped Marianne a piece of paper, without saying anything. It was the stage instructions he'd been given. Marianne pocketed the paper, planning to share it with Favre later.

Favre was back within two minutes. Marianne continued.

'That's great Kevin. You did well. You did the right thing telling us about Yves. Don't worry. No harm will come to him. If you've got nothing to hide you can tell us the rest of the story. What exactly happened that night after the show was stopped? Run us through it.'

Kevin spent the next few minutes explaining what happened, from the chapel to the menhir. Favre was impressed with Marianne. Thanks to her they now knew for sure there were *three* symbolic places they had visited that night of the solstice: the chapel, the cemetery, and the menhir.

Favre's phone vibrated again. It was Fabienne Pasche. He excused himself and left the interview room once again.

Marianne wondered whether all suspect interviews were like this. In, out, in, out. It was off-putting, to say the least. Made it difficult to maintain concentration. What was she supposed to do when he wasn't in the room?

This time she apologized to Kevin, explaining DI Favre would be back very soon. Favre returned after five embarrassing minutes.

'Mr. Gillieron. I'm going to play you the message from your Uncle B once again. Please listen carefully.'

Favre played the message on the phone.

Tell me the truth now Kevin. Was it Marco and Dani in that ambulance last night? Was it their dead bodies bumping around in the back? Did you kill them, Kevin? What did you do with their bodies?

'Monsieur Gillieron. This has now gone too far. This is what I believed happened that night. For a long time, you have wanted to harm Dani Devaud and Marco Zurcher. Why? Because they were constantly mocking you. Talking about your dad being the son of siblings. What a shame on your family! What a burden to bear! Because of this, you wanted him dead. Didn't you?'

'Sir, I would never kill anyone. Ask Marianne. I'm not like that.'

Favre was not wavering.

'You planned this murder meticulously. You realized Dani Devaud and Marco Zurcher would be attending the fund-raiser for the FC Jorat Mézières football team. You decided to drug them just before the entr'acte. As they fell to the floor on the stage, you cut all the lights and sounded the fire alarm. In the panic, and in the darkness, you opened the back door to the ambulance on stage, bundled them in, and drove off.'

'This is ridiculous.'

'You then left the mock ambulance on the parking lot, plugged it into the electricity mains, turned the temperature down to maximum freeze point – I'd say around minus twenty degrees Celsius – and left Dani Devaud and Marco Zurcher to freeze to death inside.'

Even though Favre had no hard evidence of this, he was determined to take his hypothesis to its logical conclusion. Watching all this from the observation room, Marianne could not help but feel sorry for Kevin, once again. Was Favre serious? Was he looking for a quick confession? Did he really believe Kevin to be the murderer?

Favre now adopted an even more aggressive tone. 'Mr. Gillieron. You used the ambulance to drive two other people around Servion that night for your solstice worship activities. Then, having dropped the other two persons home, you buried or otherwise disposed of the bodies of Dani Devaud and Marco Zurcher. Your Uncle B even asked you if you'd killed them. He heard the bodies moving around in the back of the van.'

Kevin was furious about such an accusation. 'Those were not human bodies, detective. They were trolleys with food. We use that vehicle as a freezer van. Haven't you checked?'

'We will be doing that tomorrow. But I'm sure you've cleaned up all the evidence already.'

'Sure I did, detective,' replied Kevin sarcastically. 'And can you tell me where I put the bodies?'

'We will find this out tomorrow. I've ordered a search of the cemetery, the area around the menhir, and the STEP - the sewage works. We would not have to do all this if you told me now precisely where you put the bodies?'

Kevin thought the whole story to be a farce. 'You have an amazing imagination, detective. Wish I had a job like yours. Then I'd get to make up stories like this one every day.'

'I'm not making this up Kevin. This is serious, and you don't seem to understand Monsieur Kevin Gillieron, I am arresting you on suspicion of the murder of Dani Devaud and Marco Zurcher. The officer over there will lead you to your cell where you will be detained for a maximum of forty-eight hours.'

Dazed by such an unbelievable accusation, Kevin put up zero resistance and was taken to his cell. It was as if he was floating around in a bad dream. But this was for real.

Chapter Twenty-Eight

The next morning, Detention cell, Blécherette, Police HQ

It was not yet six in the morning. A uniformed officer knocked on Kevin's detention cell door. He was awake. He'd hardly slept at all. The policeman entered and asked Kevin to stand up. He had a swab in his hand and ordered Kevin to open his mouth. He needed to take a sample of saliva for a DNA test. Kevin was unperturbed. He had nothing to hide.

'Go ahead officer. And could you please send me a copy of my DNA analysis, I'd like to do some ancestry research.' He was only half-joking.

'Thank you, Monsieur Gillieron. I'll bring you breakfast in a minute and the morning paper.'

'Room service isn't bad here. Think I'll come more often,' Kevin said, forcing a slight grin from the officer. 'Could I have my phone back?'

'Sorry, sir, not for the moment. The police have a limited time to charge you. They will only do this if they find evidence. If not, you'll be free to go tomorrow morning when you will get your phone back.'

'Thanks. That's what the lawyer you gave me yesterday told me. As I'm innocent, I'll be checking out tomorrow morning, then. Won't be leaving a tip, sorry.'

Ten minutes later the policeman returned with breakfast. Two croissants, some orange juice in a plastic cup, and a coffee, also in a plastic cup. No cutlery.

A copy of the day's *24 Heures* newspaper came on the same tray as the food. On the front page, bottom right was the headline, *Homage to Balthazar, thespian par excellence, page 23*. Kevin skipped straight to that page and read the obituary of his dear old Uncle B.

Thierry 'Balthazar' Bonzon takes his final bow after sixty years on stage

Monsieur Thierry 'Balthazar' Bonzon, or simply Balthazar as he was known, founder of the theatre that carried his name, passed away peacefully in his office.

96

Appropriately, the last show he organized and starred in was a fund-raiser for his local football team, FC Jorat Mézières, a team he watched with his father when he was a young boy.

Balthazar was a household name in Vaud Canton, with a career spanning over sixty years. He created the famous Servion Revue which mocked the leading politicians of the day and became the most attended show of its type in the whole canton. If you've never heard of this amazing beehive of regional culture and comedy, you can't call yourself Vaudois, such is the renown of the theatre he created from nothing.

Balthazar's brilliance lied in his ability to evolve with age and change roles in line with his physical limitations. As a young man, he hogged the leading roles, acting, dancing, and singing with increasing prowess, despite having had no professional training. Growing older, he reserved the funny and the grumpy man roles for himself and played them to perfection.

Balthazar constantly surrounded himself with highly trained, professional top-class dancers, singers, and actors, all of whom will miss him dearly, despite his sometimes-hard-handed management methods.

For Balthazar, a good boss had to be 'cruel to be kind'. His father taught him that, and he was forever thankful, as he told 24 Heures in an interview last year.

The eternal bachelor, Balthazar did not have any offspring of his own. This newspaper has it from a reliable source that Balthazar's entire estate, including the theatre and associated buildings, has been left to his second cousin, Mr. Kevin Gillieron.

Monsieur Gillieron, a message from all of us at 24 Heures and theatre lovers in Vaud Canton: KEEP UP THE GOOD WORK AND MAY THE SPIRIT OF BALTHAZAR LIVE ON FOR GENERATIONS TO COME!

Reading this, Kevin was both angry and excited at the same time.

Why me? I know nothing about managing a provincial theatre. Why didn't he tell me the other night, instead of talking some nonsense about some bodies in the back of the ambulance? How come I was the last to know?

Kevin had lots of questions that needed answering. But first, he had to get himself out of this mess that Uncle B had put him in by recording the conversation they'd had the other night.

Chapter Twenty-Nine

Same day

Cemetery, Sewage Works, Menhir, and Trash Tip in Servion

The police had spared no expense. Following Favre's conversation with Fabienne Pasche, he'd located three sites where the bodies could be buried or hidden: the cemetery, the STEP – the sewage works – and the menhir. A five-person team equipped with a mechanical digger and a sniffer dog spent the day working at each scene. Favre remained at his desk at Police HQ. He'd sent Marianne to follow proceedings and to report to him as soon as they found the bodies.

The team began at the cemetery. The digger went down to three metres around Balthazar's plot but found nothing. Marianne reported back to Favre, who instructed them to return the grave to the site they found it and move to the next site.

Next up was the sewage works. This was much more complicated. Although it had only been a few days if the bodies had been dumped in the tanks they would have decomposed rapidly. Kevin would have weighted them down, so they'd be at the bottom unless they'd gotten stuck in the pipes, which the STEP manager thought unlikely.

The easiest way to find out was to empty all the tanks. Fortunately for the team, the STEP had recently been renovated and a couple of reserve tanks had been added as overflow.

The whole process took around three hours, finishing at lunchtime. The stench was unbearable, even from a distance, putting Marianne off the wraps she'd prepared for lunch the night before. The other team members were clearly used to this, as they all ate their sandwiches without flinching.

The team found quite a few surprising objects at the bottom of the empty tanks including a motorbike and a lawnmower, but no human bodies or remains.

Next up, the menhir site.

Favre had gained special permission from the relevant authorities of the neighbouring canton of Fribourg in which the menhir was located.

The team was allowed to dig around the menhir on condition they did not touch the standing stone itself, nor destabilize the foundations.

A member of Fribourg University's Archaeological Department was present as the team went about their last task of the day.

The digger was used for the outside area around the menhir, and the team used spades and smaller tools the nearer they approached the stone.

At around four o'clock in the afternoon, one of the team members shouted '*Eureka*!' She'd found something.

The team leader went over to see what the excitement was all about. A large bone had been unearthed. Almost certainly a human femur bone. Difficult to date. There was no flesh at all left on it, ruling out Dani Devaud or Marco Zurcher – too recent.

It was getting dark quickly. The team asked Marianne to call DI Favre for instructions. Without hesitation, Favre instructed them to cover the site with a tent, set up a generator, with lighting, and to work through the night.

By three in the morning, the team had dug up what appeared to be a full skeleton of a young adult woman and man and a small baby. The bones were sent to forensics for analysis. Marianne asked the team leader if he could hazard a guess as to the age of the bones. He surmised that if the adults were alive today, they'd be in their eighties.

Marianne did some quick mental calculations. Kevin is twenty-eight. Let's say his father was thirty when Kevin was born, that makes fifty-eight. And let's suppose his parents – the alleged siblings – were in their twenties when they had Kevin's dad? That works. But who is the baby? Could that have been a second incest child? Could it have been a twin of Kevin's father, who died in childbirth?

Marianne was looking forward to the DNA tests to confirm her thoughts.

For Marianne, the excitement of working this case was tainted by sadness and uncertainty for her brother. It created a mix of emotions, flooding her brain. She just hoped Dani would knock on the door of her Mum's apartment, making some silly joke. Deep down, though, she knew this was a vain hope. Deep down, she knew he was dead. And from that same *deep down*, her instinct told her Kevin was *not* the murderer.

Chapter Thirty

The next day, Police detention cell, Blécherette, Police HQ

Kevin Gillieron slept much better on his second and final night in the detention cell.

The officer guarding the cell had taken a liking to Kevin. 'See you're getting used to the comforts of our five-star service here Monsieur Gillieron?' he joked.

'I'd like to stay for a third night, officer. And I'm sure you could you do me a discount deal. But I'm afraid I must go back to Servion to warn my second cousin he'll be having an unexpected visit today. From our lovely, warm, and friendly detective Favre.'

'Ha-ha. Warm and friendly. You bet! Have you seen the news? Looks like we've been having some fun in your neck of the woods, digging up graves, emptying sewage tanks, and finding old bones down by the menhir.'

The officer gave Kevin the day's *24 Heures* with his breakfast. He immediately read the article about searches at the Servion cemetery, sewage works, and menhir. He needed to get back home, quick.

He was released later that morning and went straight to Yves Graff's farmhouse, opposite the chapel on the hill in Servion.

As he arrived at Yves's farm, he saw an old *Opel Antara* outside. With a magnetic blue gyrophare on the roof, driver side. A doctor? Kevin entered the farm from the backdoor, straight into the kitchen. He knew the house well. Yves had said he could always enter via the back, around past the cowshed, and through an old wooden door. He made it to the kitchen of the old, somewhat decrepit farmhouse, and heard a conversation taking the front room. Instead of moving through he decided to eavesdrop from the kitchen. No mistaking: it was DI Favre questioning Yves about the night of the solstice.

'What time did Kevin Gillieron pick you up to take you down to the cemetery, Monsieur Graff?'

'We met at the chapel first. Must have been about one in the morning, I guess?'

'You guess? I need a precise time, Monsieur.'

'Yes, sure inspector. It was one a.m.'

'What did you do in the chapel?'

'We carried out our standard worship ritual and then drove down to the cemetery, where we carried out the same procedure, and then again at the menhir. It's the same every solstice and equinox. It's our tradition. We've been doing it for hundreds of years. Kevin was driving.'

'Was he driving the mock ambulance that was used that evening on stage at the theatre.'

'I believe so, yes.'

'Our eyewitness said you and Thierry Bonzon - we assume it was him with you - were wearing masks. We need to sequester one of these to take to the police station for identification.'

'No problem. I'll go upstairs and fetch one.'

Worried that Yves may see him in the kitchen, Kevin hid in the large old pantry where Yves kept his vegetables and other perishables. He remained there for a few minutes while Yves got the masks for DI Favre. Glancing at the shelves he came across a small box. He looked inside and saw some old invoices. These must be for the meat he delivers to Servion zoo, Kevin thought.

Looking through the invoices Kevin recognized the names of several local farmers he knew who slaughtered their old cows and sold the meat to Yves. And then he saw an invoice from a name he also recognized: Dirk de Clippele the football agent. It was for some meat he delivered on three different occasions over the past six months.

This made Kevin think. Why would one of Europe's most successful and richest football agents be selling meat to a local wholesaler in a small Swiss village? Unless there was another person with the name of Dirk de Clippele selling meat in the area, it must be the same de Clippele who had signed Granit, Dani and Marco.

Yves had returned to the front room with the masks for Favre. Kevin decided he'd seen and heard enough, and left the same way he arrived, pocketing the invoices from Dirk de Clippele.

As he got to the front of the house, he took his car keys out of his pocket. But instead of going to his car, he walked towards Favre's Opel Antara. Placing his ignition key between his thumb and his front finger, he pressed the tip of the key against the paintwork of the Antara and made as deep an indent as his strength allowed, along the full length of the car, passenger side. *Sweet!*

Chapter Thirty

On the same day, afternoon

While DI Favre had been interviewing Yves Graff at his farmhouse, Marianne had spent the morning with the police search team finishing off their work at the menhir. The bones of the adult male and female and baby were taken away for forensic analysis. Favre needed to know both the age of the bones as well as the likely cause of death, presuming there was sufficient evidence. With no overtly visible injuries or fractures to any of the bones, and no other elements dug up at the site, this could prove difficult to ascertain.

After the interview with Graff, Favre met Marianne at the menhir site. Following a thorough site inspection, which revealed nothing new, he told Marianne it was her *lucky day*. He'd pay for lunch at *La Croix Fédérale* restaurant in the nearby village of Essertes.

It was past midday, and the restaurant was fully reserved. Not a free table in the whole place. To Marianne's great surprise, Favre showed his police badge to the restaurant manager and, *hey presto*, a table was found straightaway. Magic.

Once seated, Marianne inquired. 'I don't mean to be impertinent, but isn't showing your police badge to get a table *abuse* of your position?'

Favre seemed completely unfazed. 'Don't you worry about that, young woman. You'll learn with time. Now, tell me what you know about the search teamwork.' The *young woman* reference grated Marianne, not for the first time.

'There's nothing more to add since yesterday. Old bones, probably sixty to eighty years old. No obvious fractures. No obvious cause of death. It will take some weeks for the full analysis to come through. How did your interview go with Yves Graff?'

'Seems he's legit. Took time, but he finally opened up. He gave me one of the masks they wear for all that devil-worshipping stuff.'

'Boss, I think it's more like sun-worshipping.'

'Whatever. Heathen, pagan stuff.'

Marianne remembered that Favre was not only the son of a protestant pastor, but he was also the husband of one. Would that explain his judgemental attitude?

'Any more information on Graff, boss?'

'He's got a side-line business that is generating much more income than his farming activities. He buys old carcasses from local farmers, freezes them, and sells the meat to the local zoo. He recently invested in some industrial freezers at the back of his cowshed. Smart guy.'

Marianne was immediately suspicious. 'Good place to hide dead bodies, no? Shall I dig deeper? See what he keeps there?'

'Nah. As I say, he's legit. He did say he throws some old dog and cat meat and bones in with the overall mix. That's illegal, I know. The fact that he owned up to this tells me he's being open and transparent. In any case, we'd need a search warrant. I think we've caused enough upheaval in this small village for the present.'

'If you say so, boss. Still, I think that's a line of inquiry that we should follow up at the appropriate time.'

'Sure, Marianne. Made your choice?'

'I'm going for a big salad. And you?'

'The rabbit stew, *à la moutarde*. Looks delicious.'

'Better check it's not from Graff's freezers, boss.'

'I always thought you had a good sense of humour, Marianne. Good. In our line of work, it helps.'

Marianne refrained from laughing.

'What about Kevin Gillieron, boss?'

'What about him?' Favre replied, lips pursing.

'With respect, boss, I don't think he is our man. Did Yves say anything about the noise in the back of the mock ambulance that night of the solstice?'

'I asked him. He said he didn't hear a thing. That doesn't mean Dani and Marco weren't already there, freezing to death.'

Marianne cringed and looked away for an instant.

'Sorry, Marianne. That was insensitive. Forgot Dani's your brother. My apologies.'

Favre finished his meal before Marianne was halfway through her salad dish, which she could not finish in any case. The thought of Dani, frozen in the back of that vehicle, had dimmed her appetite.

'Let's go, boss. I need some fresh air.'

Favre paid with his police credit card, and they walked to the car in silence.

As they reached the car, Marianne saw something. 'Come, look, boss. Not nice.'

Favre came around to the passenger side and saw the long, deep scratch which ran across the two side doors to the front headlight.

Favre was furious. 'The bastards.'

'How do you know there is more than one person? Seems to me to be the work of one key, held firmly in one full movement, from back to front.' Marianne was trying to bring some rationality to her observation. 'In any case, your insurance should cover this, shouldn't it?'

Favre stared at Marianne, almost accusingly. 'No, Marianne. Remember this is my Opel *Poubelle*. Not worth having more than the minimum coverage on an old car like this.'

'Well, boss, it certainly looks more like a *Poubelle* now,' she joked.

'Not funny, young woman. Get in the car. We need to get back to HQ. There's an urgent matter I need to attend to.'

Even though there was no specific emergency warranting it, Favre put the flashing gyrophare on the roof of his scarred *Poubelle* and raced back to Blécherette. No further words were exchanged for the whole twenty-minute journey.

Chapter Thirty-One

Four weeks later, February 2nd, La Blécherette, Police HQ

Four weeks had passed since they'd had that lunch together in the small village of Essertes, next to Servion. Since then, Favre had become increasingly cold and distant towards Marianne. Perhaps she should have said nothing about the car scratch. It was as if she'd scratched the car herself, the way Favre had looked at her and ignored her most of the time.

Or maybe it was because they had made no real progress on the Devaud-Zurcher case. They were both still officially *missing*. In Marianne's mind though, they should be put into the *presumed dead* category.

Marianne had made her views known to DI Favre. She said she did not think that Kevin could have killed her brother and Marco Zurcher. He was not capable of murder. But for Favre, Kevin was still a suspect.

The case was at an impasse.

Marianne had lapsed back into her natural sleeping rhythm and was arriving at the office later and later. That morning she did not get in until nine-thirty. Walking past her desk for what was probably his fourth or fifth coffee, Favre threw out a sarcastic *good afternoon young lady*. Not to be outdone, Marianne replied *yes, it is a lovely afternoon, isn't it boss?* Favre then said that she was wanted in her office in five minutes.

Expecting to be reprimanded for her brazenness, Marianne was surprised that Favre had brought her a coffee too.

'Sit down Marianne. I need your help this afternoon. It's Balthazar's funeral. Yes, I know. A month seems a long time to keep the body in the morgue. But Kevin Gillieron insisted. Today, February 2, is the midpoint between the winter solstice and the spring equinox. That's how he wanted it. Don't ask me why.'

'Where does it take place?' Marianne tried to sound as if she didn't already know.

'Don't humour me, Marianne, I know you know. The temple in Mézières. I want you to go. Listen in. Pick up on the local gossip.'

'Will you be going, boss?'

'Yes. But not with you. We'll operate separately for this event, Marianne.'

'Can I catch a ride with you, boss?'

'OK, but I'll drop you off in Servion, before Mézières. Don't want anyone seeing us arrive together.'

'Servion? It's a three-kilometre walk to the church from there.'

'You'll figure it out.'

'Guess I've got no choice. Did you get that scratch on your car fixed?'

'Not yet. I'm looking for a low-cost repair shop. Know anyone?'

'Sure. Paul Porchet. He has a bodywork garage just opposite the theatre in Servion. I can have a word with him today if you like. He'll be at the funeral, for sure. He knew Balthazar well. You can drop me off there.'

Marianne was wondering whether Favre would invite her for lunch before running her to Servion. No such luck. He had sandwiches delivered and ate them alone in his office. She skipped lunch, knowing there would be plenty to eat and drink at Balthazar's wake at the theatre, after the funeral service in Mézières. She was looking forward to it, in a weird way. Funerals are often more fun and relaxed than weddings, she thought. Less visible stress. Less expectation.

What sort of surprise would Balthazar have reserved for his final curtain call, she wondered?

Chapter Thirty-Two

Servion, Paul Porchet's garage

DI Favre dropped Marianne off at Paul Porchet's garage.
Paul was in his mid-fifties. A gentle giant of a man. Here she knew she was in friendly territory. Paul had fixed her mother's car on several occasions. Marianne knew how much Paul, a widower, fancied her Mum. She thought they'd make a good match, despite the big difference in height between the two. Neither had made any conclusive moves so far, but she'd a sensed a strong mutual interest.
Her plan was simple. She'd get Paul to drive her to her mum's flat in Mézières. They'd have a coffee there, and then go to the funeral and wake together at the theatre, the three of them. She also had a secondary plan. Favre needed his Opel *Poubelle* repainted. Maybe Paul could do him a special price. A win-win situation for all, no?
Paul took the bait perfectly, agreeing to everything Marianne requested. A kind man.

They arrived at her mum's apartment with plenty of time to spare. As Marianne had predicted, her mother was very pleased to see Paul and invited him in for a coffee and some cake. Paul offered his regrets about Dani being missing and took her mum's hand in his. She did not let go for many seconds. While they were talking, Marianne went into her brother Dani's old bedroom to snoop around. She didn't know precisely what she was looking for. Favre had taught her to always be on the lookout for *stuff*. *Stuff*, he said, leads to clues, which lead to suppositions, which can lead to the identification of suspects, which lead to culprits, which lead to convictions.
She looked under his bed. On top of his wardrobe. In his drawers. Nothing of note. She then went through his books. He had all seven *Harry Potter* books. She took them out, one by one, not knowing why. Dani had purchased each book upon release. They were all hardbacks. She flipped through each book until she reached *Harry Potter and the Order of the Phoenix,* the thickest of the seven J.K. Rowling tomes. She could not believe what she saw inside. Dani had taken an exactor blade and cut

out a large square of paper in the middle and hidden an old iPhone 5 inside. Why had he done that?

She took the phone out and turned it on, but the battery was dead, and she didn't have the right charger with her. It would have to wait until she got home that evening. She put all the books back on the shelves and left the room as she had found it.

When she went back into the lounge, she saw Paul with his arms around her mum on the sofa, consoling her, saying that he was sure Dani would turn up sooner or later.

Chapter Thirty-Three

Early afternoon, Mézières Temple

Good thing they arrived early. The church was packed, and there was an overspill of people onto the car park. Marianne and her mother on Paul Porchet's arm, found places on the back pews, on the upstairs balcony. The service was due to begin at two-thirty in the afternoon. People were already in their places at two p.m. knowing this would be Balthazar's last sell-out event. From her seat, Marianne could see DI Favre sitting alongside Fabienne Pasche. Waiting to commence proceedings, Pastor Véronique Favre had taken her seat next to the coffin, which was already in place at the altar. Kevin Gillieron and Yves Graff were seated on the second row, reserved for family members, with Balthazar's two sisters and their families seated in the front row. Marianne felt for Kevin, as he said one final farewell to his Uncle B, who'd been a father figure since his dad had committed suicide.

Suddenly, without warning, the emergency sirens in the village started to wail. Of course, remembered Marianne, it was February 2nd, the day in Switzerland all emergency sirens across the country are tested. It was also the mid-point day between the winter solstice and the spring equinox. Coincidence?

Back at the zoo in Servion, the wolves began to howl. They did this each time the emergency sirens were tested, every February 2, believing the sirens to be the howls of fellow wolves somewhere close by! To top it all, in the USA February 2 was the famous *Groundhog Day*. Marianne recalled watching the movie when she was a kid. Could old Balthazar have planned all these coincidences? The theatrics were certainly perfect for his final send-off. Balthazar must be howling in heaven, or would he have preferred hell, Marianne pondered?

In addition to a large contingent from the Servion and Mézières municipalities, quite a few dignitaries from the Vaud Canton were present including the cantonal minister for education and culture and the heads of some bigger city theatres, most of whom had looked down disdainfully upon Balthazar's *popular* productions. They were there because the Minister for Culture was there, to lobby her for more money later, at the post-funeral reception at Balthazar's theatre.

The service lasted just thirty minutes. Pastor Favre read from the New Testament, St Paul's first letter to the Corinthians. A beautiful text on the power of love. Kevin Gillieron gave an emotional eulogy, praising Balthazar's vision and courage. He also thanked his Uncle B for the confidence in transferring the ownership of the theatre. To finish the *show*, as Balthazar would have called it, three dancers and a singer from the theatre troupe rendered a stirring performance of *Life is a Cabaret*, in English. The words rang so very true for the life of Balthazar.

Start by admitting
From cradle to tomb
Isn't that long a stay

Life is a Cabaret, old chum
Only a Cabaret, old chum
And I love a Cabaret

Apart from Fabienne Pasche and Philippe Favre, Marianne could not see a dry eye in the whole church. Her mother was sobbing like a baby, with Paul consoling her.

After the service, most people went to Balthazar's Theatre. It made sense to have the wake there. There was ample parking, and the kitchen was big enough to cater to a few hundred guests. Within minutes Marianne had steered Paul Porchet and his mother towards DI Favre, who was his wife Véronique and the Syndique, Fabienne Pasche.

'Mrs. Favre, boss, Madame la Syndique. Sorry to interrupt. I'd just like to thank the Pastor for a very poignant ceremony and *adieu* to Balthazar.'

Véronique Favre was genuinely touched. 'Many thanks. It's always delicate with celebrities. Good to see you, Marianne. My husband speaks very positively about you, don't you Philippe?'

Philippe Favre looked away; Marianne blushed.

'I'd like to introduce your husband to Paul Porchet. He owns the bodywork car repair shop in Servion.'

Paul, duly warned and appropriately briefed, stepped forward and shook Philippe Favre's hand. 'Pleased to meet you. At your service.'

Véronique laughed. 'Must be something to do with his Opel *Poubelle*, I guess? Don't know why he holds onto that old-timer when his position at the police gives him the right to a new car every three years. Nostalgia, I suppose?'

Her husband gave her a look that said *leave me alone with Paul Porchet, I need a favour.* Véronique sensed the moment and invited Marianne's mother and her to get some refreshments. Fabienne Pasche also moved on, with Madame la Syndique in full meet-and-greet mode for her constituents, leaving Porchet and Favre alone.

'Opel *Poubelle*,' Paul laughed. 'That's what we say in the trade. It's not true, of course. I own an Opel myself and it's never broken down. What's more, it's such a common brand, nobody wants to steal it or vandalize it. I read a statistic the other day....'

'Well, that's just the problem, Mr. Porchet. Some stupid idiots *did* vandalize my car. A month ago, here in Servion, while I was parked opposite the chapel on the hill. A long deep scratch the whole length of the car. And my insurance doesn't cover it.'

'Sorry to hear that. Can't think who in our tranquil village would want to do that. It's not even a police car.'

Paul then realized what he'd said. 'No worries. Leave it with me, detective. Let it be my small contribution to the valuable work of our valued police force.'

'That's very kind of you. Most appreciated.' Favre thought he'd better make some small talk before moving on to search for *stuff*. 'So, did you know old Balthazar?'

'Very well. He was a good customer. He was always getting into small accidents. A great actor, director, and theatre manager. But driving? Not his *forte*. I'd sort out his prangs and he'd give me complimentary tickets for the shows.'

'I see.' Favre was about to move on when Paul said something that made him think again.

'I painted that mock ambulance used in the fund-raising show for the FC Jorat Mézières. I took the standard design and colours of the local ambulances. Yellow and blue with red lines on the back door. I even painted the 144-emergency number on it. Complex job, I can tell you that. Took me a whole week.'

'Tell me more about this, I'm curious.'

'I did it for free. My way of supporting local culture. That Dirk de Clippele fellow. The football agent. Balthazar told me he purchased it uniquely for the theatre from the catering company in Oron-la-Ville. Nice gesture, I thought. It's a freezer van. Practical, no?'

'When was this?'

'A few months ago. He came here with the president of the football club, Coach Weymo they call him, another one who can't drive.'

'Can you describe the vehicle to me?'

'Just a standard catering van. Closed-back compartment. You can't access it from the front seats, that fit three persons. No window to check what's happening in the fridge compartment in the back. You must use the wing mirrors to see what's behind.'

'Do you know Mr. Kevin Gillieron, Mr. Porchet?' Favre asked, as politely as he could, without wanting to appear threatening or accusatory.

'Kevin? Everyone in this village knows Kevin Gillieron, detective. I've fixed a couple of cars for him as well.'

'Many thanks for your time, Mr. Porchet. I appreciate your offer to fix my car. I'll drop it off tomorrow. Thanks again. And if you think of anything else regarding that mock ambulance, here's my card. Call me.'

Porchet watched Favre leave. Five minutes later, he remembered something. Should he call? Nah, it wasn't really that important.

Chapter Thirty-Four

Same day, evening

Marianne got back to her apartment in Lausanne at seven p.m. Back to work. She immediately plugged Dani's old iPhone into the charger. Turning it on, she realized she needed Dani's password. This time she didn't have a face to use, even if old Balthazar's was a dead face the last time she broke into a phone. She had three attempts. She racked her brain. When did he use it? Was it when he was playing for the Swiss under-eighteen team? Didn't they win the UEFA Championship in Spain that year? It's got to be that! He was saying it all the time. *Hop Suisse*. She entered the first six letters, *HopSui*. It worked.

She went straight to the photo file. There was no order. Dani had used this mobile for three years, so there was a lot to sift through. It was mainly football.

She clicked on the video section. Her family on vacation in Gambia, on the beach, splashing in the water. Another one of the Swiss team in the coach in Spain. And then she opened another video. Dani was filming ahead of him, walking along a beach, moving the camera from right to left, then down to his bare feet. Spain again? A full ten-minute clip. Left towards the sea, then right towards the sea wall, and back straight ahead. It was as if he was looking for something, or someone.

She saw the insignias of a couple of hotels and figured this must be Sitges, where Dani's team stayed that year. The video was boring. Why was he doing this? For the first few minutes, she heard what appeared to be Marco Zurcher's voice, though she could not make out his words, which were smothered by the sound of the wind and sea.

She was about to stop just as the video focused on two men lying side by side in the distance. Dani had zoomed in on them. He got closer and closer, keeping the zoom fixed on the two men. After a few seconds, they began to kiss. Marianne recognized one of the men. It was Granit Berisha.

Chapter Thirty-Five

The next morning, Police HQ, Blécherette

The next morning, for the first time in four weeks Marianne arrived at her desk before her boss, at six-fifteen a.m. She couldn't wait to tell him about the video she'd found on her brother's phone. A *sex tape*, her first! She wasn't sure what it meant, or if it related in any way to Dani and Marco's disappearance. But DI Favre would certainly dismiss this and reiterate his hypothesis that Kevin Gillieron was still hiding something important.

They met over coffee in his office. It wasn't that Favre was *not* interested in the video. He just didn't see the relevance to Dani and Marco's disappearance.

'All this proves, Marianne, is that Granit had a bit of a flirt with a man in Spain when he was eighteen years old. No big deal. Who cares? Didn't you read about Granit's marriage to Miss Kosovo a few years ago? Lucky man.'

'With respect, boss, that could be a marriage of convenience. What if Granit is hiding something? How many openly gay footballers can you name?'

Favre scratched his head. Marianne quickly realized it was a dumb question. He probably couldn't name *any* straight or gay footballers.

Marianne continued. 'What I'm saying is that Granit's marriage to Miss Kosovo could be a way of disguising his true sexuality. Happy families, and all that! They have a daughter, but who's to say that Granit is the father?'

'You're fabulizing, Marianne. Even if you're right, how does that connect to the disappearance of Dani and Marco? Or their potential deaths? Remember, we need *motive*. The only person who we've so far identified with a strong motive is Kevin Gillieron. And I'm sure he's still hiding something from us.'

'Again, with respect boss, I don't think Kevin is our man. He may have hated my brother for ribbing him and being nasty about that incest stuff, but I don't see him as a killer.'

'Keep focused, young woman.'

Marianne bit her tongue.

'What motive would Granit have to kill Dani and Marco?'

'I don't know boss but give me some time and I'll come back to you,'

'OK. But not too much time.'

'Thanks, boss. By the way, how did your discussion go with Paul Porchet yesterday?'

'Very well. He proposed to fix up my car. At no charge. He also told me he painted the mock ambulance used on stage.'

'So, he's not a suspect, then?'

'At first, I thought he could be. That whole village seems to know each other, and half are inter-related. I wondered whether he could be involved in this solstice nonsense. Then I figured not.'

'Why not, if you don't mind me asking, boss?'

'He seemed too transparent to me. Copper's nose, and all that. You'll develop that as well, over time.'

'So where do we go from here?'

'We wait. Something will turn up. It always does. Mark my words, young woman.'

Young woman, again! Marianne hated him for calling her that. Such a chauvinist. And he's not yet fifty years old. What will he be like when he's an old man?

'What should I do with that video, boss?'

'Want to make a hundred thousand francs? Sell it to the highest bidder. Don't even look at the Swiss media. Go straight to the gutter press in the UK. They'll give you very good money for that. It will wreck Granit's career, of course, but you'll be richer.'

'Are you serious, boss?'

'I've seen a lot of nonsense in our newspapers here in Switzerland. But the UK media are the most unscrupulous in the world. They make our papers like *Blick* seem as tame as a lamb. Up to you.'

Marianne thought a while. 'No thanks, I'll keep it to myself. I'll copy it to the police server in a secure file and give you the password.'

'Sounds good. Look, I've got to get on with some work. Keep digging. *Stuff* will soon float to the surface. Always does.'

Chapter Thirty-Six

Later that week, Friday morning

Like Favre, Paul Porchet was an early bird. He'd been working in his garage for one hour when DI Philippe Favre turned up at seven that morning to pick up his Opel Antara, his beloved *Poubelle*. Paul showed him the repair job he'd done. Better than new. He had resprayed the whole side. Beautiful work.

'Monsieur Porchet, I can't thank you enough. I know you said you would not take any money from me. So instead, here is an envelope with two tickets to the next show at Balthazar's.'

"That is very kind of you detective. Much appreciated. I'll ask Mrs. Devaud, Marianne's mum to come with me.'

'I see. Good for you. I won't say anything to Marianne, or her mother. Surprise, eh?'

'I'm a widower, you see, and it's taken me a long time to get back into the game.'

'Fingers crossed for you. My old dad is a widower too. My mother died when I was ten. Not easy to bring up kids on your own.'

'Detective. Can I tell you something?'

'Sure, fire away.'

Favre was wondering if he'd made a mistake to mention his family history. Perhaps Paul was looking for a soulmate to talk to, and he was certainly *not* that person.

'That freezer van I re-painted as an ambulance.'

Favre was immediately relieved Porchet didn't want to get *personal*.

'Yes, what about it?'

'Well, detective, I don't know whether it's relevant or in any way important.'

'Go on,' Favre said, looking at his watch, thinking he should be getting to work now.

'A couple of weeks after I'd finished that paint job, I had a call from a bodywork garage in Liège, Belgium.'

'Belgium?' Favre asked.

'Yes. The garage owner wanted me to send him the *exact* specs of the freezer-van-come ambulance. He'd been asked by a client to find the same model and to make an identical replica, right down to the finer paint details. With only one difference. His vehicle was a four-wheel-drive version.'

'Did you send him anything?'

'I did. By email. The paint pantones, the brand, the typeface to the wording, the whole lot. Over thirty pictures in all. He was very insistent.'

'Do you still have the email correspondence? If you do, please send it to me immediately.'

'I will. Do you think it's relevant to the disappearance of Dani Devaud and Marco Zurcher?'

'Too early to say. We'd certainly like to speak to this man. Did he say who his client was?'

'I didn't ask. Didn't seem important.'

'Anything else that comes to mind? Anything other strange happenings linked to the ambulance re-painting?'

'Again, detective, I don't know whether this is relevant.'

'Try me.'

'That rich football agent who paid for the freezer van that I converted into the ambulance.'

'Dirk de Clippele?'

'That's him. He was the person who collected the ambulance when it was finished to take it to the theatre. Not very far, is it? Just across the road. Well, I watched him as he left. He didn't take it to the theatre. He kept on driving towards Mézières.'

'What did you do?'

'I thought it was strange. So, I jumped into a car, and followed him, from a distance.'

'Where did he go?'

'Down the main road, then off to the left, past the funny-looking castle-type house with turrets, down to the derelict farmhouse, and then into the woods.'

'Did you follow him into the woods?'

'No. It was a dirt track, and I didn't want to get the expensive Mercedes dirty. It was a customer's car.'

Favre wondered why Dirk de Clippele would want to explore the local woods. He needed to find connections.

Chapter Thirty-Seven

Same morning, Restaurant La Croix Fédérale, Essertes

Happy to be back in the driving seat of his rejuvenated Opel *Poubelle*, DI Favre called Marianne, from his mobile phone, hands-free.

'Marianne. Get uniform to run you to the same restaurant we had lunch that time in Essertes, *La Croix Fédérale.*'

'I wondered where you were, boss. I've been here since six a.m. I have some new information. It's important. Hot *stuff*, boss. I talked to Paul on Wednesday and…'

'Keep it for when you get to the restaurant. The place will be empty at this hour. I'll find a discreet table in the corner.'

Thirty minutes later Marianne was sitting opposite DI Favre at a table in a dark corner of the restaurant in Essertes, close to Servion. The landlady of the establishment remembered them from the last time they were there. This time she was thinking differently. Is this an *older man, younger woman, situation?*

The landlady added biscuits and cake for free to the two coffees Favre ordered. They began to exchange information, Marianne went first.

'I stopped by Porchet's garage yesterday for a chat. He told me Dirk de Clippele had visited him at his garage.'

'I know, Marianne. De Clippele purchased the freezer van Porchet repainted as a mock ambulance for the football club fund-raiser.'

'Yes, but what you don't know is this. Porchet also told me Mr. de Clippele asked him to find a full *camouflage cover* for the mock ambulance.'

'A camouflage cover for the stage ambulance? Why?'

'Exactly. Porchet had no idea why, and he didn't ask. He's too nice.'

'Maybe he's just polite, with good manners, not wanting to meddle in anyone's affairs. Did he find one?'

'He did. At the military surplus store. De Clippele picked it up the day before the show at the theatre. What about you? What's your new information?'

Favre explained what Porchet had said to him early that morning about the replica order from Belgium.

'Why would someone want a complete replica of the ambulance used on stage?' Marianne asked.

118

'And that someone has a bodywork shop in Liège, Belgium. Think about it, Marianne. Where does Mr. de Clippele come from?'

'Belgium. Of course. It's beginning to make sense. Not too sure he ever lived in Liège, though.'

'Belgium is a small country. Even smaller than Switzerland.'

'His dad owned an abattoir in Antwerp. Dani told me. Dirk worked there and did his apprenticeship as a butcher, when was eighteen. I can do some more research about him, boss.'

'Definitely. Do that when we get back to the office. I want to know *everything* about him.' Favre said as he broke off a piece of cake. 'Want some?'

'Thanks. Looks tasty.' Marianne was not being polite. She was staving, having skipped breakfast to get to the office early that morning.

'Let's get our heads around this. Why did Dirk de Clippele want a second ambulance? And why did he drive into the woods? Is there anything interesting there? Any connection?'

'When I used to worry about my figure, I used to do the *Parcours Vita* in that neck of the woods. I used to run past the famous *Grottes de Pendens* in the *Riaux Woods*, near Mézières. Never been there, boss?'

'No. Guess if you don't grow up in these parts you don't get to see all those hidden-away places.'

'There are two grottos there big enough to hide an ambulance.'

'Let's go there now.'

'Sure. Would you like me to drive the *Poubelle*, boss? You could sit comfortably in the back and admire the beautiful *Jorat* countryside.'

Marianne was joking, of course, and expected a typically condescending reply from Favre.

'Sure, Marianne. Here are the keys. Hope your feet reach the pedals.'

Marianne returned the joke. 'Let's go, boss. I'll use cruise control to give my legs a rest.'

Ten minutes later they were at the derelict farmhouse on the edge of the *Riaux* woods, next to Mézières. Marianne stopped the car and got out. She quickly opened the back door for DI Favre before he could get out on his own.

'Thank you, James.'

'My pleasure, your honour. We should walk from here, boss. This is where Porchet parked his car and observed Clippele driving down the dirt track towards the grottos. Maybe we'll find car tracks? It's a long shot, I know. The lumberjacks don't access the forest from this point, and neither do the farmers. We'll probably find some mountain bike tracks, though.'

The two of them walked slowly on the muddy track leading up to the grottos. There were three or four car tracks for the first two hundred metres. Then only tracks from one vehicle for the next hundred metres leading up to the first grotto. The mock ambulance would have passed, just.

Favre took pictures of the car tracks with his phone. He would send these to forensics. They entered the first grotto. Big enough to hide a car at the back, where there was a dip. Passers-by would have to look hard to see it, but with the right *camouflage*, it would blend nicely into the rock.

Marianne started looking for *stuff*. Favre continued to take photos with his phone.

'Boss, look at this.'

'Don't touch! Use your plastic protective gloves!'

'I didn't bring any.'

Once again, Marianne knew she'd given him another wonderful opportunity to patronize her.

'Lesson number one. When out in the field, at a potential crime scene *always* take your notebook your protective gloves, and plastic container. You should know that *young woman*.'

'My apologies, boss. Could I use yours?'

Favre looked in all his pockets and didn't find his gloves nor a plastic container. He'd come straight from his home that morning to Porchet's garage not anticipating he'd be out in the field at a potential crime scene that day.

'Stay here.'

Marianne remained at the grotto while Favre ran back to the car. He returned with the requisite gloves and container. He picked up the two cigarette butts she'd found on the floor of the grotto. No mistaking the brand. *Davidoff Slims.*

Chapter Thirty-Eight

Two days later, Sunday evening

Kevin Gillieron was sitting in his Uncle B's office at the theatre that Sunday evening. He'd never been much of a drinker, but since his arrest and detention, he'd started drinking whisky. His Uncle B kept a stock of top-quality Scottish single malts in a glass cupboard in his office, and he was beginning to acquire a taste for them.

Kevin had not been charged with anything, having been the prime suspect and having spent two nights in the Police HQ detention cell. He was angry. His reputation had been damaged. People at the Servion Municipality were talking about him behind his back. Some thought he'd committed a crime. No smoke without fire.

The Syndique, Fabienne Pasche, had started to look at him differently. With a more suspicious eye. His apprentice too. And when he was working at the tip, he saw people staring at him as if he were an animal in the zoo.

When Kevin first learned from the *24 Heures* newspaper that he'd inherited the theatre, he'd thought he'd stay in his job with the Municipality and hire someone experienced to manage the theatre. No more. Not the way people were looking at him at work. His plan had changed. Now, he wanted to be respected by his peers, instead of being talked about behind his back as a suspected murderer. And to begin with, he must get a *public apology* from the police. Where to start?

Marianne. Of course. She was the solution. He had to get Marianne on his side. She could help him get that apology.

It was eight in the evening. Not too late, Kevin thought. He picked up his mobile and called Marianne. Her number was on speed dial.

'Marianne. It's me. Kevin. Look, I know you may think I'm still a suspect, but I can promise you on the tombstone of my father's grave that I have *nothing* to do with the disappearance of your brother and Marco. Believe me.'

'I do, Kevin. That's what I told DI Favre. That's why he let you go.'

'No, Marianne. The reason I was released is because there is no evidence to accuse me of anything. I am INNOCENT.'

'You are Kevin. Now, I must go. I'm making dinner for my boyfriend. He's on his way, after his shift.'

'A cop. You're with a cop? Suppose it's more exciting than being with the municipal employee like me?'

'That was a long time ago, Kevin.'

'I'm joking.'

'Doesn't sound like it?'

'Don't be so arrogant, Marianne.'

Marianne was a little taken aback. This was not the sort of aggressive language Kevin used. Being arrested must have toughened him up.

'Sorry, Kevin. Look, I've got to go.'

'Don't hang up. I've got something for you.'

'What?'

'I can't tell you over the phone. It could be important in your search for Dani. Or for the search for his killer.'

'How do you know that?'

'Trust me, Marianne. Come down to the theatre, now.'

'I'll come with my boyfriend.'

'No. Just you. On your own. Otherwise, I won't give you this piece of very important evidence. Does the name Dirk de Clippele mean anything to you?'

'Sure. He's Dani's football agent.'

'That's your clue, Marianne.'

Marianne was not afraid of Kevin. She just didn't want to be alone with him. She knew deep down he was still very fond of her. Such a shame. He's a handsome man, and not that stupid. He'd make some local girl very happy, surely. And he's beginning to toughen up, even if his jokes were so *paywai*. She decided to go.

Marianne arrived at the theatre to find all the lights in the foyer off, and the front door locked. She was about to go back home when Kevin arrived from a hidden door and invited her directly into his office. This was the first time she'd been there since she saw Balthazar dead in his chair, the same chair Kevin was now using.'

'Whisky? I've only got single malts.'

'Do you have a beer?'

'Sure. I'll have to go around to the theatre bar to get one. Just give me a minute.'

While Kevin was fetching the beer, Marianne had a quick snoop around the office. This was becoming a habit. She didn't know precisely what she was looking for. *Stuff*. She didn't have time to look in the office desk drawers but did manage to go through Kevin's jacket pockets before he returned with a cold beer from the local *Jorat* brewery. Nothing of interest in the pockets, dammit.

'Thanks, Kevin. Tell me, to what do I owe this pleasure. What is this amazing piece of evidence that is going to help me find my brother?'

Kevin opened the lower drawer of his office desk, pulled out a piece of paper, and handed it to Marianne. It was an invoice.

'Take a look,' Kevin said.

Marianne studied the invoice. *Yves Graff Frozen Deliveries*. Three-thousand and forty-three Swiss Francs, payable to Dirk de Clippele. It had the date and precise time of delivery, from last year.

'So?' At first, Marianne did not see any particular significance in the receipt. She knew Yves Graff was now running a successful business supplying Servion zoo with meat. So what?

'Look again. The name.'

Then it clicked.

'Dirk de Clippele is an extremely wealthy football agent. Why would he supply meat to Yves Graff?'

'That's exactly what I thought?' Kevin replied.

'How did you get this?'

'I can't tell you.'

'Come on Kevin. I cannot use this unless I know where it came from. It must be authenticated. We must know where you found it. The precise location.'

After a few minutes in silence, Kevin decided it was wiser to tell Marianne all that had happened the day he was let out of his detention cell and visited his cousin Yves Graff's farmhouse.

Marianne thanked Kevin for his honesty and transparency. She would follow up on the invoice for de Clippele. She sensed, though, that something was missing.

'Is there anything else you'd like to tell me, Kevin?'

'No. Well, yes. Only if you promise to keep it a secret.'

Marianne said it would depend on the importance to the case of what he was about to tell her.

'It was me. I did it.'

'You did what, Kevin? Think about what you are about to say before you say it. It can be used as evidence against you.'

'I scratched Favre's car. Revenge, you see. What an asshole that man is.'

At this point, Marianne let out an enormous, raucous laugh.

'You scratched the *Poubelle*? Hahaha! No worries, Kevin, your secret is safe with me.'

Marianne had got what she'd come for. She thanked Kevin, gave him the obligatory three pecks on alternate cheeks, and said *adieu*. Until next time, which she hoped would not be that soon.

She could not wait to tell her boss about this new *stuff* she'd dug up. Not bad for a Sunday night.

Chapter Nine

Blécherette, Police HQ, Monday morning

Philippe Favre was not normal. Marianne knew that. Was he, perhaps, a little autistic? Asperger's, perhaps? He certainly liked his routine. Then again, he could be impulsive and improvise, as he did the Friday before. Maybe he was just stubbornly OCD.

That morning, early, both DI Favre and Marianne Devaud parked their cars at the same time on the same lot that, at six-thirty a.m. They both walked towards the lift. Favre got there first, pressed his badge, and the lift door opened. Marianne rushed into the lift behind him.

'Morning boss. Good weekend?'

Favre did not even acknowledge Marianne's presence, never mind reply. His eyes remained fixed on the lift door. It was as if he were in another world. A trance. As if he never expected to cross Marianne in the lift so early in the morning. Because that had never happened before in his morning routine. His brain wasn't ready. It hadn't been pre-alerted. Was that a sign of Asperger's, Marianne wondered as the lift ascended?

Marianne could feel herself blushing, blood running up to her face, heating it, without warning. She looked away from her boss. Arriving at their floor, Marianne went directly to her desk, Favre to his office. They were the first ones to arrive that morning.

Around fifteen minutes later, when three other people had arrived, Favre came from his office out to Marianne's desk. It was as if he'd never seen her earlier.

'Good morning, Marianne. Can you please come to my office? I'm getting a coffee. Want one?'

In his office, Favre took Marianne by surprise again.

'Good weekend?' He very rarely asked her that. Marianne tried to forget what a weirdo he was and started talking.

'Very productive, boss. Look what our friend Kevin Gillieron gave me.

Marianne handed the invoice Kevin had given her the previous evening, from Yves Graff to Dirk de Clippele for the meat he'd sold.

Favre twigged immediately. Dirk de Clippele, *again*. Now he's selling meat! The dots were beginning to become more numerous. The problem was connecting them.

'Thanks Marianne. Good work. I'm going to re-focus our investigation on Dirk de Clippele. I've no idea why he would want to sell meat to Yves Graff. As far as I know, Yves has just one customer: Servion zoo. What sort of meat is he selling, and why? In this case, the *why* is more important than the *what*. On Friday I asked you to do some research on de Clippele. What have you come up with?'

Marianne had forgotten about Favre's request. Instead of admitting this, she decided to improvise, from what Dani had told her over the years about this wealthy football agent.

'Absolutely, boss. You probably know that Mr. de Clippele is a well-known football agent. He signed three players from FC Jorat Mézières when they were kids: my brother Dani Devaud, Granit Berisha, and Marco Zurcher. Granit is now worth around ten million Swiss Francs to Mr. de Clippele each year.'

'That much?' Favre asked.

'Probably more, boss.' She was thinking on her feet, as she was speaking. 'I suggest we look into the relationship between the President of the FC Jorat Mézières club, Ray McCauley, and Mr. de Clippele.'

'Why, Marianne?

'Ray McCauley – or *Weymo* as he's known at the club – coached the three players picked up by Dirk de Clippele.'

'Do you think he got a cut of de Clippele's fees, or commissions, or whatever? I don't know much about football wheeling and dealing. Prefer ice hockey.'

That was good news for Marianne. She could wing it, from what she'd learned from her brother.

'It's complicated boss. According to FIFA rules, an agent cannot be paid for his services if the player is under the age of eighteen. Once a contract is made, it cannot last for longer than two years. My brother Dani renegotiated his one with Mr. de Clippele every other year. Each time he got transferred, de Clippele got ten percent of the transfer fee. Not bad. Think of how much he'd get if Real Madrid make an offer of three-hundred million for Granit Berisha?'

'Loyalty, both ways, is vital. It can be win-win, or lose-lose, I guess.' Favre was trying to be smart.

'You've got it. Loyalty is key. Boss, if you allow, I'll put all the information I have on Mr. de Clippele into a report and email it to you first thing tomorrow morning.'

That would give her all night to do some proper research.

'Sure. Let's do that. In ten minutes meet me in the third-floor operations room. I've called a meeting and need to brief the larger team I formed for this case. I'll be asking you to give them a summary of their progress so far. See you there.'

Marianne returned to her desk, pleased she managed to wing it, but worried she had just ten minutes to prepare her summary to the new case team.

Nine minutes later she was in the operations room with five other colleagues who had all been asked to join the new team that DI Favre had created.

Favre kicked off.

'Ladies and gentlemen. Welcome to *Operation Last Seen*, the case of missing persons Dani Devaud and Marco Zurcher. They have both been missing since the night of the fund-raising event for FC Jorat Mézières a couple of months ago at Balthazar's theatre in Servion. We have had no trace whatsoever of these two persons, both professional footballers, since then. I chose my words carefully. I say fateful because we must now assume they are dead. Had they been kidnapped we'd have surely received a ransom note by now. Marianne Devaud, whom you all know, has been helping me with this case. She is the brother of Dani Devaud. Normally we would not allow her to work on the case, but I got clearance from the head of the cantonal police. She has already added considerable value to this inquiry. Any questions so far?'

There were none. DI Favre continued.

'What do we know so far? Devaud and Zurcher were last seen on stage at Balthazar's Theatre just before the blackout during the entr'acte. Like fellow footballer Granit Berisha, they were both dressed up as Santas. And so were two other people, one of whom is the central focus of our investigation, Mr. Dirk de Clippele.'

An older detective, with a red, alcoholic face, who looked like he was already past retirement age, piped up. 'Who was the fifth Santa, boss?'

'Good question. It was Anita Patel, de Clippele's lawyer. For the moment she is not a prime suspect. However, we always keep our minds open to any eventuality, don't we?'

Favre said this as a teacher would speak to a class of eleven-year-olds.

'Marianne Devaud will continue with the briefing from here. Over to you, Marianne.'

This was the first time Marianne had addressed a crowd of seasoned and experienced detectives. She was visibly nervous. She'd been jotting down her thoughts on the piece of paper she had in her hand now. It was wavering, as she trembled, so she put it down and spoke from memory.

'Thanks, boss. Yes, Dani Devaud is my brother. And yes, I want to get the person or persons who, I believe, killed him along with Marco Zurcher. And yes, I am one hundred percent capable of discernment and objectivity in this case. Allow me to thank Detective Inspector Favre and the head of our cantonal police for their confidence in me.'

She took a sip from the bottle of fizzy water on the table and continued.

'As DI Favre explained, they were last seen on the stage of the theatre at the entr'acte. They were there for the lottery competition. The audience was asked to identify each player as they walked across the stage disguised as Santas. The last two to go were Dani and Marco, sorry, Devaud and Zurcher. They both staggered across the stage, as if they were drunk or had been drugged, and fell on the floor. Then the lights went out.'

The same red-faced detective interrupted with another question. 'How do you know that it was Dani and Marco on the floor, and not Granit Berisha, Mrs. Patel, or Mr. de Clippele?'

'Good question.' Marianne said this but didn't mean it at all. In fact, it was a stupid question. 'Mrs. Patel and Mr. de Clippele and Granit Berisha, were all found safe outside the theatre, whereas there has been no trace of Devaud and Zurcher since.'

The detective insisted.' Sure, but it could have been Berisha and Patel pretending to have been drugged, who knows? Have you questioned them about this?'

'We will do, for sure. Allow me to continue. The next day, when I got to my mother's house where I'd left my mobile phone, I immediately accessed my voicemail. Let me now play this message back to you. Please not that it was recorded around forty-five minutes *after* the blackout in the theatre.'

Marianne put her phone on loudspeaker and played the voicemail.

Help Marianne. No joke. Think…drugged….drinks. Can't….the. ….scared. Freezing in here. Don't …die. Help. Quick…..now…..soon.

Marianne continued. 'You can hear that the message is cut up. Maybe the signal was weak. This could that be consistent with him being stuck in the back of a van, disguised as the ambulance on the stage of the theatre, and driven out during the blackout?'

Favre paused for a moment to let his new team think about that, then took the lead again.

'That ambulance was donated to the theatre by Dirk de Clippele. The driver of the vehicle, which also doubled up as a freezer van for food deliveries to the theatre, was Kevin Gillieron. He is employed by the Servion municipality. He was our original suspect. He was also spotted later that evening driving that ambulance. He's now been cleared, though I think he's still hiding information.'

Favre paused again.

'So, you may ask why we are now switching our attention to Mr. Dirk de Clippele? Marianne, please explain.'

Marianne stood up again and started to speak. She was gaining confidence.

'There are four important pieces of information and evidence that suggest Mr. de Clippele is involved in the disappearance of Messrs Devaud and Zurcher. Firstly, we believe he had a replica ambulance made at a car bodywork shop in Liège, Belgium, his home country. I will be able to confirm this later this week when I visit the garage. Secondly, we have a witness who saw Mr. de Clippele drive into the woods, near some grottos, where we found some evidence, including some *Davidoff Slims* cigarette butts. Thirdly, we've found out that Mr. de Clippele supplies Yves Graff's freezers with meat destined for the zoo in the village.'

As Marianne was saying this, she realized just how skimpy and unconnected that evidence was. The red-faced, older detective evidently thought the same.

'Boss, with respect, this all seems very tenuous. Perhaps these three elements are purely coincidental?'

Marianne continued, ignoring the question.

'Finally, the fourth element is this.'

She got out her phone and share the screen onto the TV monitor in the conference room, via Bluetooth.

'What you are about to see is *highly confidential*.'

Marianne played what was now being unjustly called the *sex tape*.

'One of the men on the beach is Granit Berisha when he was eighteen years old in Sitges, Spain.'

Favre then summed up. He explained they think there is a connection between these four bits of information; that Mr. Dirk de Clippele was strongly involved, and maybe even the killer. And that it's now our job to connect the dots.

'Tomorrow, Marianne will travel to Belgium to interview the owner of the Liège garage. We've already contacted the Belgian Police. Later, I will fly to Liverpool to interview Granit Berisha. Why is he still alive and Dani Devaud and Marco Zurcher missing, presumed dead? Thank you, team. Your individual tasks are clearly outlined in the files in front of you. Let's get to work.'

Chapter Forty

The following day, Tuesday, Granit and Emina Berisha's house in Caldy, Wirral, near Liverpool, England

Their house was now finished. Since the last time Dirk and Anita visited, Granit and Emina had added an indoor swimming pool, as well as a spa with a sauna and hammam.

It was contract renewal time. Anita had sent Granit's lawyer the updated version, with the new conditions. A large video-gaming company wanted to purchase Granit's *avatar* for its soccer products. Naturally, Dirk wanted a cut from this as well as from a biography of Granit that *Liverpool Post* editor, Sanjay Singh, had proposed to write. There was nothing untoward with the new contract, apart from one clause.

Granit's lawyer had picked up on this immediately. Instead of the standard two years duration, the new contract had no specified renewal or termination date. What's more, Dirk's commission and cut of the transfer fee had increased substantially. Granit's lawyer had sent him an email explaining all of this, copying Emina Berisha. Granit left Emina to manage his email correspondence, and she had not replied, nor had she told him about these new conditions.

They were all seated in the enormous lounge, with a beautiful view of the river Dee and over to the Welsh hills when Granit's lawyer came straight out with it.

'Mr. and Mrs. Berisha, it is my duty to advise you *not* to sign the new contract.' Granit asked why, and his lawyer explained that it was against FIFA rules to have a contract between a player and an agent that was more than two years' duration.

Granit replied that it was surely up to him to decide that, and not FIFA, the international football federation. Surely, FIFA was wrong. Dirk had represented him all his life, and he was happy to sign a new contract with no renewal date.

His lawyer did not understand. Granit had complained vociferously to him only six months ago about Dirk de Clippele, his agent. De Clippele had still not completed a specific and *very important* task Granit

131

had ordered him to do. Unfortunately, Granit did not explain to his contract lawyer what, precisely, he'd asked de Clippele to do.

Given Granit's total change of attitude, his lawyer now assumed that de Clippele had finally carried out his promise to Granit, whatever that may have been. Granit signed the new contract without even reading it. It appeared that Granit had found total confidence in his agent, once again. A complete turnaround from the situation six months ago.

His lawyer would have loved to have known *why*, but realized it was not his place to ask. He was just the lawyer. He left promptly to attend to another footballer client, a small-time League Two player at the end of his career with local team Tranmere Rovers FC.

The four who remained had lunch together out on the heated balcony, after which Dirk decided to accompany Granit to his training session in Kirby, leaving Anita and Emina to catch up.

Emina had never explained to Granit that it was Anita, not Dirk, who had played *matchmaker* role for them. Granit didn't need to know. They both knew and understood *why* they were together, and the secret was safe all around. They fully respected each other's roles and gave each other the necessary space. Their daughter was now about to turn six. She was looking more and more like her biological father Luigi, who lived in Milan, where Emina modelled regularly. She took her daughter with her on most occasions, along with their Italian nanny.

Emina was eternally grateful for what Anita had done for her. The arrangement with Granit suited her perfectly. She knew it was only temporary, and she'd explain it all to her daughter when she was much older. Luigi had his own family in Milan and Emina knew deep down he would never leave his Italian wife. Anita exploited this gratitude to the maximum. Emina had agreed to send her regular updates, including texts between Dirk and Granit. Today was update and upload day for Anita.

Knowledge is power. Anita needed to know everything about her lover, Dirk de Clippele. For, despite being one of his very few *confidantes*, he kept his secrets well-hidden. Just as she did.

Chapter Forty-One

The same day, Tuesday, Liège, Belgium

As Granit was signing his new contract with Dirk de Clippele, Marianne Devaud had arrived in Liège, Belgium, for lunch with the owner of the garage who had created a replica mock ambulance to the one used on stage at Balthazar's Theatre.

Marianne had driven from Lausanne, setting off at four in the morning for the seven-hour drive. She'd take an unmarked police car as she didn't trust her old Peugeot not to break down. The garage owner had accepted her offer of lunch. The Belgian police had been notified of her visit and would also be present. She'd planned to drive back via Strasbourg that evening, where she'd stay the night with an old Lausanne university friend, who'd married a French medical doctor from that city.

The garage owner, a gruff man in his late forties, had a Flemish name, Janssens. Marianne was expecting hostility. Mr. Janssens had refused to disclose the name of the person who'd ordered the painting of the replica ambulance. It was only when DI Favre threatened to involve the Belgian police that he agreed to be interviewed, but only with the presence of a Belgian police officer.

Over lunch, Mr. Janssens warmed up and seemed to take to the pretty young Swiss girl. He explained to Marianne how his family were originally from Antwerp and had moved to Liège a couple of generations ago. Back then the French-speaking part of Belgium was richer than the Flemish. He'd inherited the garage from his father, who had serviced the vans and trucks used by de Clippele's family business, which delivered meat all over Belgium. The two families knew each other well. He also gave Marianne the precise dates of the paint job he'd done for de Clippele.

Marianne was grateful for this information. 'Thanks for your transparency. I realize it can't be easy to open up to strangers, like me, from foreign police forces. I'd like to reassure you that Mr. de Clippele is *not* in any way a suspect. And there is no need to inform him of our visit.'

As soon as these words came out of her mouth, she regretted saying them. Mr. Janssens laughed. 'You've come the whole way from Switzerland to question me about a person who is *not* a suspect? Give me a break! Let me tell you this, Madame. Dirk de Clippele is an honest, upright man. Just two weeks ago he returned that same ambulance to us. He sold it back to me for a knock-down price. A true gentleman. I re-painted the vehicle and sold it on. I'll send you all the details via email. I thanked him for his generosity. And yes, before you ask, I'll send you all the details of the new owner.'

As he said this, Mr. Janssens looked at the Belgian policeman for approval, who dutifully nodded.

Marianne continued. 'Just one final question. Mr. Janssens. Were the tyres on the ambulance Mr. de Clippele returned to you the same as the ones on it when you sold it to him?'

'Yes, why? It was a four-wheel-drive. He'd specially asked for tyres that would grip well in the snow and the mud. I'll send you the brand by email. That's because I'm a friendly, cooperative Belgian, aren't I officer?' Janssens looked again to his compatriot, who dutifully replied with an approving nod.

'Many thanks again, Mr. Janssens. You've been very helpful. Gentlemen.' Marianne stood up, shook their hands, and went to the bar to pay the bill. She was glad to be on her way. She could not help feeling they were looking down on her, the *little Swiss*. For once, *she* was the one who felt like the *paywai* today. *Note to self: be nicer to Kevin next time you see him.*

In less than four hours' drive, she'd arrived at her friend's apartment in central Strasbourg. She loved this city. She was here just three months ago with her new boyfriend Kenosha for the Christmas market. Beautiful. It had been their first road trip together, taking in all the scenic old medieval villages that ended with *Heim*, the prettiest being *Eguisheim*, where they'd had the best *choucroute* dish ever. That was what she was aiming for tonight. DI Favre said it would be ok for her to use the police credit card to pay for a reasonably priced meal for her and two guests, given that she was saving on a hotel room.

They found a cozy restaurant on the canal in the medieval part of the city. It could have been Amsterdam. Or Bruges. All three chose *choucroute* and washed it down with Alsatian beer from a local brewery recommended by her friend's doctor-husband.

Marianne had intended to ask him some delicate questions related to the disappearance of her brother and Marco Zurcher. She wasn't too sure whether it would be appropriate at the table while they were eating but fired away all the same.

'If you wanted to drug someone so that they are not completely K.O., but under your control, what substance would you use?'

The doctor-husband said there were many options. The one he saw most in his work was the well-known date rape drug, *scopolamine*. As soon as he said *date rape drug*, Marianne knew what he was talking about. Women of her generation regularly shared information on social media about this horrible drug used by predatory men on both women and men, mainly in nightclubs. A friend of hers had been a victim quite recently.

When the three of them got home, Marianne asked politely if they would be interested in hearing her *hypothesis* for the case she was working on. She had not told anyone about this yet. Not even Favre. It was almost too horrific to be true. Favre would have certainly called her a fantasist, again. She wanted to test this hypothesis before confronting him with it. And her friends in Strasbourg were sufficiently distanced from the case to be valuable guinea pigs.

Chapter Forty-Two

The next day, Wednesday

DI Favre left his Mézières home at four in the morning. His flight to Liverpool was at seven. Liverpool FC was playing a UEFA Champions League match against Barcelona FC that evening. Granit Berisha was injured, so would be available for the interview that a Liverpool police officer by the name of DI Steve Whittley had set up at Merseyside Police HQ in the city centre.

He had a window seat. It was a clear morning. The plane flew directly over Paris. Looking down he could make out the *Arc de Triomphe* and the roads that led away from it, in a star-shaped fashion. It was clear the whole way across the English Channel. As the plane passed the south coast, the clouds came in. The landing at *John Lennon* airport was weird. The plane emerged from the clouds and landed almost instantaneously; the clouds were so low in the sky. Favre had visited England several times. This was the first time he noticed just how close to the ground the clouds were stuck, almost touching it.

Walking down the steps of the plane he was struck by the high level of humidity. It wasn't raining, but he felt wet all the same. DI Whittley met him on the tarmac and whisked him through some private gate like a VIP, though he did have to show his passport.

The Merseyside Police HQ was close to the renovated docks and the riverside, which had become a UNESCO World Heritage Site. Granit Berisha was waiting for him in the plush, well-appointed office of the Police Chief Constable on the sixth floor, with a magnificent view of the river Mersey. She was the highest-graded member of the police force there and had welcomed Berisha to the building earlier.

The Chief Constable herself introduced Granit Berisha to Detective Inspector Philippe Favre, in the presence of DI Steve Whittley. She then left the office, repeating that they could use it for as long as they needed.

Favre had only spoken English to his hosts, a language he rarely had to opportunity to use these days. In the car from the airport, DI Whittley had complimented Favre on his excellent English, saying it reminded him of Nelson Mandela. Favre explained how he'd lived in Botswana as a kid, where he'd learned both the Tswana and the English languages.

DI Whittley stayed with them throughout the two-hour interview. Favre called it a discussion. Whittley closely observed the Swiss officer's interview techniques, even if he only understood ten percent of the conversation, which was in French. Just as Whittley would have done, Favre began by playing the good and gentle cop, then gradually turned the screws.

After thirty minutes he'd ascertained from Granit Berisha that Coach Weymo, who everyone at FC Jorat Mézières adored, was not that adorable after all. Berisha said he had *proof* of payments being made from Dirk de Clippele to Coach Weymo from the time the *Brio Trio* had been picked up by Lausanne Sports FC, when they were just fourteen years old. This was illegal. He said he was still receiving monthly payments from Dirk de Clippele to this day.

Favre decided it was time to turn the first screw.

'Granit Berisha. Can you confirm this is you in this videotape?' From the mirror-screen option on his phone, Favre projected the video that Dani Devaud had taken on his phone of Granit with another man on a beach in Sitges, Spain when he was eighteen.

Watching this, Granit became furious, very quickly. 'Where did you get that? You have no right to have that video. It's private. And you don't have the right to show it to anyone else in this room.'

'Mr. Berisha. You have not answered the question. Is that you in this video?'

Granit was red-faced, mad and feeling more threatened.

'So what? Does it matter? That was then. This is now. Yes, I experimented with my sexuality. No big deal, is it? I'm married now and I've got a daughter. She looks just like me.'

'Mr. Berisha. We are not here to judge you or anyone else. We do not care one little bit about your private life. As you say, no big deal. We are here to discover the *truth* in missing persons case back home in Switzerland. We believe you will be able to help us with our inquiries.'

'And do I get to know what this case is all about? Isn't it my right to know?'

'Let me tell you right now.'

Favre spent the next few minutes explaining how Dani Devaud and Marco Zurcher had not been seen since the night of the FC Jorat

Mézières fund-raising event at Balthazar's Theatre, which Granit also attended. Surely Granit had heard this news, he asked?

Granit replied that his life was *so* busy, he had no time for news or gossip. Emina had not mentioned it, and he didn't read any Swiss newspapers. His news came primarily from social media and there had been no mention of this disappearance on his feeds.

He was still fuming. 'Where did you find that video? I have a right to know?'

'I'm not too sure that you do have any legal right to know. We found that video. It came up in our search for evidence that might help us find Dani Devaud and Marco Zurcher. Alive, we hope. Or dead. And I think you know very well where we found it, don't you?'

'No, I don't. Why would I ask the question?'

Favre decided it was time to go for the jugular.

'Mr. Berisha. We have evidence to prove that your agent, Mr. Dirk de Clippele, was directly involved in the disappearance and perhaps the murder of your former teammates, Dani Devaud and Marco Zurcher.'

Granit said nothing.

'We believe that Mr. de Clippele acted on *your* orders. And we also believe he is blackmailing you. He knows something that you don't want the police to know. Is that right?'

Favre was trying his luck with this statement, as it was pure supposition, with no evidence to back it up.

This time Granit replied. 'That is the most ridiculous thing I've ever heard. Wait until I tell my wife about it. She'll have our lawyer sue you for defamation.'

Favre was not going to get into that argument now. He knew Granit had no legal recourse to do this. Nevertheless, he was interested in his reaction.

'We won't need to speak with your wife today. However, we reserve the right to do this at any point in the future.'

DI Favre had one more question for Granit Berisha.

'Apart from a few weeks ago in Servion when the famous *Brio Trio* were together for the fund-raising event at the theatre, when did you last see your friend Dani Devaud, Mr. Berisha?'

'My friend?'

'Isn't Dani a good mate of yours? You grew up together. Friends from a young age. Played together on the Swiss team. No longer your pal? Why not?'

'Must be five years ago. He interrupted a dinner I was having with my agent and his lawyer.'

'Dirk de Clippele and Anita Patel, right?'

'Yes.'

'Mr. Berisha. Did Mr. Dani Devaud try to blackmail you that evening?'

'Why would he want to do that?'

'I think you know, Mr. Berisha. It was Dani Devaud who filmed you on the beach in Sitges, wasn't it? Kissing another man.'

'I honestly don't recall, and none of that matters anymore. Not to me.'

'So, if Dani were to sell this videotape to the press, you wouldn't mind, would you?'

'Look, detective. As I said before, that was then, and this is now. You don't seem to be listening to me. I'm done. This interview is finished. I came here in good faith. And now, in that same good faith, I'm leaving. Have a good day.'

Granit got up and left the room. He took the stairs down, calling his chauffeur along the way to pick him up immediately.

Back in the Chief Constable's office, DI Favre looked over the table to DI Whittley. In his Mandela-like accent, he said 'Thoughts?'

Steve Whittley's reply came quickly. 'The man is hiding something. No doubt, in my opinion.'

'My thoughts too. Thanks again for all your help.'

'You're welcome. I'll have uniform drive you back to the airport. Sorry, I can't take you there myself. I've been invited to the VIP lounge at Anfield tonight. One of the better perks of my job. I've been a Liverpool supporter since I was a kid. Safe travels back, and remember, *You'll Never Walk Alone.*'

As they parted, DI Whittley gave DI Favre a couple of small gifts. He said he hoped they would remind him of the great city of Liverpool, and its glorious football club: a Liverpool FC cap and a pair of LFC branded sunglasses. Favre thanked Whittley, wondering all the same why anyone would ever need sunglasses in Liverpool.

Chapter Forty-Three

The same week, Thursday, Police HQ, Blécherette

Marianne had not gone into work the previous day, preferring to work online. She'd returned from Strasbourg around midday, wrote up the report of her visit to Liège, and emailed it to DI Favre that evening. Her reply confirmation showed he'd opened it just before midnight.

She got to work at seven a.m. the next day, expecting to see Favre's car in his parking spot. She'd promised herself never to repeat the weird experience of sharing the lift with him. His car was not there. Good. All clear. Perhaps he'd allowed himself a lie-in, after his Liverpool trip. She arrived at her desk only to see that Favre *was* there, seated in his glass-panelled office reading. From closer up, she saw it was her report.

She entered his office, without knocking. Favre had told her some time ago that she didn't need to knock when she saw her was alone. Nevertheless, he seemed annoyed she had entered so abruptly.

'Good morning, boss. Did the *Poubelle* break down? Somebody scratched it again?'

She could see that Favre was not sharing her light-heartedness.

'Flat tyre this morning,' Favre replied.

'Bad luck,' she replied, trying not to laugh. 'Had time to read my Liège report, boss?'

'Yes, I have. Seems that Dirk de Clippele is much more involved than we previously imagined. Good work, girl.'

'Thanks,' Marianne replied, thinking it must be the first time he's ever congratulated her. Next time, though, drop the *girl* bit, you male chauvinist, condescending and patronizing pig.

'Where does that take us now, boss? And how was your interview with Granit?'

'Granit Berisha is still hiding *stuff*. I felt it as did my Liverpool colleague, DI Whittley. We'll need to speak with him again. He told us Ray McCauley, the President of FC Jorat Mézières, has been receiving money from Dirk de Clippele. Lots of money, for many years, and he's still getting some. I want you to investigate this, Marianne. We'll need to find a judge who'll authorize permission to examine his bank accounts over the past fifteen years.'

'That could take some time, couldn't it, boss?'

'Yes, which is why I also want you to call this number, and don't tell anyone. She's my inside contact at the cantonal bank. We don't know if McCauley has his accounts there. If he does, my contact will give you some *advance* information while we await the judge's decision.'

'I'm on it,' Marianne replied, not sure if bypassing the judge was legal.

'We also need more granularity about what happened at the theatre that night.'

'Granularity, boss. What's that?'

'More detailed info, Marianne. We know that Kevin received *different* instructions than the rest of the stage crew. How did this happen? And why? Did Balthazar hand out the instructions personally? Or was it someone else? Ray McCauley? Dirk de Clippele? Speak with Kevin again. You did keep the stage instructions Kevin gave you, didn't you? Remember? When we interviewed him, and he confided in you?'

He's got the memory of an elephant, Marianne thought.

'Yes, but I never thought to ask the other members of the stage crew? I'll get onto that as well, boss.'

'Let's have a de-brief after lunch. That should give you enough time.'

'What about doing it over lunch? Away from the office. This time, my treat. I'll book a discrete corner table again. Le-Mont-sur-Lausanne?'

'Well, that would be very kind of you. Much appreciated. I'll meet you there. My car is being delivered here at lunchtime, to the office. Paul Porchet is taking care of it again. Good man, that Paul.'

The next three hours were fast and furious for Marianne. Favre's bank contact confirmed that Ray McCauley – *Coach Weymo* - was a customer. And yes, in addition to his monthly salary from the Lausanne Hotel School, his account showed regular payments from a company headquartered in Luxembourg. No mention of Dirk de Clippele. This didn't surprise Marianne. She was sure de Clippele was smart and had different aliases, hiding behind offshore companies in different jurisdictions.

She called Kevin mid-morning.

'Kevin. It's Marianne Devaud.'

'Marianne. Guess you're calling about the apology I'm waiting for?'

'I wasn't, but we can talk about that as well.'

'As well as what?'

'We're still doing some research around the stage instructions that you received. We'd like to know whether the paper you received was different from the one the other stagehands received. I'll need to talk to some of your employees who worked that night.'

'No need, Marianne, I've figured it all out myself. I can tell you. But only when Favre has apologized to me. That's the condition.'

Marianne knew it was going to be difficult to get her boss to do this. 'Kevin. I didn't say anything to him about your scratching his car. Is that not enough revenge for you?'

'No, I need an apology. For my reputation and personal pride. No apology, no information.'

Marianne said she'd call him later in the day. She hung up and tried to figure out how to make this work.

Over lunch she briefed DI Favre on her morning's findings, stating she suspected Ray McCauley was not declaring the income he was receiving from Dirk de Clippele to the tax authorities. She then broached the apology question.

'Boss, this is delicate.'

'Go on, I'm all ears.'

Marianne hesitated. 'Would you agree that in our line of work *the end justify the means?*'

'Definitely. For example, if we get a confession by spinning yarns with a suspect, that's ok. The storytelling is justified by the confession.'

'What about apologizing?'

'Never apologize. Never explain. Too complicated in our line of work. Only as a last resort. Or if we are legally required to do so.'

'And if the success of a case depends on it?'

'Maybe, maybe not. Why are you asking me this?'

'I spoke with Kevin Gillieron this morning. He told me he has some more *vital* evidence.'

'Good. Then he has a legal obligation to hand that evidence over to us.'

'He will. On one condition. You apologize to him.'

'No way, Marianne.'

'Please. What have you got to lose? Your pride? Remember the saying, *pride goeth before a fall?* Old Testament, I think. Book of Proverbs. As the

142

son of a pastor and the husband of one, I'm sure you know it, boss. We can do it by video call. It will be a lot easier than in person. And quicker. On condition that he gives us his evidence.'

Impressed by Marianne's knowledge of the bible, Favre relented.

'I don't like it, but I will go along with it. Just this once.'

'Thanks, boss, you won't regret it. No time like the present. In my car. It's in the restaurant parking.'

Favre was uncomfortable with the idea of sitting as a passenger in Marianne's beaten-up old Peugeot. He was worried about being seen by his colleagues.

'OK, but I want you to sit in the back and keep your head down.'

Marianne paid the bill for lunch. It made her feel good, even if she couldn't afford it. They went to her car, and she lay low on the small back seat, with her boss in the front.

Marianne called Kevin with the camera on. He replied immediately.

'I'm waiting Marianne.'

'I'll pass you over to DI Favre.'

Favre took the phone. For some strange reason, he'd put his LFC sunglasses and cap that DI Whittley had given him. Perhaps this helped him feel more incognito, more distant. The apology was quick.

'Mr. Gillieron, on behalf of the cantonal police please accept our sincere apologies for the way we treated you.'

No more. No less. Having done this, Favre gave the phone directly back to Marianne.

Kevin did not reply. Instead, he moved away from the camera. Marianne wondered if he'd gone somewhere. He came back after a couple of minutes. It looked as if he'd had tears in his eyes.

'Sorry, Marianne. Just went out to get the evidence I promised you.'

'Thanks. What is it?'

'I'll email it to you. A stagehand who was with me the night Dani and Marco disappeared. She kept her copy of the instructions and gave it to me. It's *completely different* from the one I received.'

'In what way?'

'Uncle B always used a template on his PC with the words *Break a Leg, in English*, at the bottom right of all his written communication.'

'And?'

'And, on the instructions I received there was no *Break a Leg* signature. This means it they came from someone else, not Balthazar.'

'Any ideas who, Kevin?'

DI Favre was recording the conversation on his phone as they spoke.

'Yes. It was Dirk de Clippele. He was in the foyer area when the instructions were handed out. Uncle B remained seated as he was having problems with his hip. Dirk handed the sheets out to all the stagehands. But he forgot me. When the others left, I asked Uncle B for my stage instructions, and Dirk got up to give me them.'

Marianne interjected. 'Are you sure that it was Dirk de Clippele? Would you be prepared to confirm this under oath in a court of law, Kevin?'

Kevin hesitated a few seconds. He then said *Yes*.

Marianne thanked Kevin, explaining that this evidence and his acting as a witness could be vital to the success of the case. She asked DI Favre to remain in the car while she explained her *hypothesis* to him, the one she'd tested on her friends in Strasbourg.

At the end of her narrative, Favre looked totally flabbergasted.

'It's a long shot, Marianne. If that's true, if that's how it was done, it is one of the cleverest and most horrible murder cases I've ever worked on.'

Chapter Forty-Four

The following day, Friday

Anita Patel arrived at Geneva airport from London City that Friday morning at ten a.m. As usual, she'd told her husband she'd be visiting their children at their exclusive boarding school in Switzerland. She would see them, of course. But not until after she'd spend a passionate night of champagne and lovemaking with Dirk at his place in Coligny, Geneva.

Normally, Dirk sent his trusted chauffeur to pick her up. This time he drove himself. Earlier that morning he'd had a call from Mr. Janssens in Liège informing him of the visit from the Belgian and Swiss police. He needed to align his story with Anita's in case the police questioned them.

The fifty-minute drive to the airport took him through the city of Geneva. Enough time to catch up on his phone messages, hands-free in his Tesla. Five minutes into the journey, a call came up on the screen. It was Yves Graff. Dirk took the call.

'Mr. Graff. What a pleasure. What can I do for you?'

'Mr. de Clippele. Sorry to bother you. I know you're a busy man. Just wanted to know if you had any meat supplies you could deliver? I guess you're still in that business?'

Dirk didn't know what to say. He needed to think fast.

'Mr. Graff. I told you the meat I delivered last time was surplus from my family abattoir business in Belgium, didn't I?

'You did. And I was very grateful. Supplies are not always reliable from my farmer friends here in the Jorat region. And we've have had an issue.'

'What issue? Maybe I can help?'

'There is a nasty rumour going around that some of the product I supply to the zoo contains domestic pets. Cats and dogs. The police are saying there are some unscrupulous veterinary clinics in the region that have sold the meat to some of my farmer suppliers. Everyone denies everything, of course. The upshot is that a police forensics team will be carrying out DNA tests of the excrement from the animals at the zoo. The ones which are fed with my meat supplies.'

Dirk was now thinking faster. 'Mr. Graff. Would you be so kind as to tell me when the meat I last delivered was dropped off at the zoo? I can assure you, it was definitely not cat or dog meat.'

'The batch you delivered went to the zoo earlier this week, Mr. de Clippele. I remember because it was a whole frozen mishmash of beef, goat, sheep, horse and pig. All finely cut up. That batch will have probably gone to the boars. They eat everything, including the bones.'

'Do you know when it was given to the boars?'

'No need to worry about that, Mr. de Clippele. As you say, there wasn't any cat or dog in the batch. I'm not worried about how they will trace *your* supplies, which are above board. Wish I could say the same about some of my local associates.'

Dirk would have preferred a more precise date but decided not to push further.

'Mr. Graff, I'm sorry. I haven't yet answered your question. Unfortunately, there is no meat surplus available at present from our family business. Next time, I hope. Good luck with the DNA testing.'

'Thanks Mr. de Clippele. Have a good day.'

Dirk had to move quickly. Whatever plans Anita may have for the weekend would have to be jettisoned. They needed to be smart. They needed to keep their wits about them and *be aligned*. That was essential.

Anita sensed something was wrong because Dirk did not get out of the car to greet her when he arrived at the airport. That had never happened before. She got in the car. She moved over to kiss Dirk, but he looked straight ahead, started the car, and drove, direction Lausanne.

It was only when Anita lit up a *Davidoff Lights* cigarette that Dirk spoke. 'Throw it out of the window. I hate smoking.'

'Nice to see you too, *big man*. Fell out of the wrong side of the bed this morning? That same bed where I always have a smoke after lovemaking? What's up?'

'I'm going to drop you off at the service station on the *autoroute* near Nyon.'

'Got a meeting at the UEFA offices, have you? I thought this was going to be our special night. Just the two of us.'

'You will then be driven to your chalet in Villars-Sur-Ollon. You can spend more time with your kids this weekend. Please don't interrupt me until I've finished what I have to say.'

Anita was now worried, almost frightened. She'd never seen Dirk like this. She followed his instructions and didn't say a further word, as he explained to her what she needed to know about the ongoing police inquiry. He finished by asking her to repeat exactly what their *aligned* story would be, should they be interviewed by the police. Anita did this, almost word for word; her legal training had equipped her with an excellent memory.

At the service station, Anita transferred to the other car. No kisses. No goodbyes. And Dirk had instructed no *personal* communication until further notice.

Back in his Tesla, Dirk called Coach Weymo, who picked up immediately. He was at the FC Jorat Mézières training ground, watching the first team prepare for an important match that evening.

'Dirk. Long time, no see. All good?'

Dirk and Coach Weymo spoke in English. Dirk was in no mood for banter or gossip and got straight to the point. 'Have the police contacted you?'

'No, Dirk. Why would they? Is there something I should know?'

'The only thing you should know, Weymo, is to keep your dumb mouth shut. I've been paying you good money for many years now. Much more than you ever deserved. And you will not say a word about any of this if you are questioned. Understand?'

Coach Weymo was taken aback. This came completely out of the blue. No warning.

'No problem, Dirk. You can trust me.'

'There will be consequences, if not. Make no mistake my friend.'

Weymo felt a chill go down his spine. The man was not joking. Dirk continued. 'Tell me, do you know anything about a videotape that Dani Devaud took of Granit in Sitges, at the under-eighteen European Championship in Spain?'

He assured Dirk he did not know anything about that at all. Dirk had not finished.

'Weymo, listen carefully. There will be no more financial transfers. However, I am prepared to give you one final payment, in cash. Twenty purple notes. On one condition. I need you to do me a favour. It's just one night's work.'

Weymo thought for a few seconds. A purple Swiss banknote was worth a thousand francs. Probably the most valuable banknote in the world. Twenty-thousand Swiss Francs for one night's work?

'Sure, Dirk. I'm in. What's the favour?'

Chapter Forty-Five

The following week, Monday morning, Police HQ, Blécherette

Favre gathered the *Operation Last Seen* team together at eight o'clock that morning. He and Marianne briefed the others about their findings from their trips to Liège and Liverpool. Favre summarized what they now knew for sure.

'Firstly, de Clippele sold fresh meat to Yves Graff, a supplier to the Servion Zoo. We know this because of the invoices Kevin Gillieron found in Graff's house. We need to know *why* is he selling meat to Mr. Graff?

Secondly, de Clippele commissioned a second replica ambulance to the one used on stage the evening that Marco Zurcher and Dani Devaud disappeared. Why?

Thirdly, Granit Berisha admits there was a potentially compromising video made of him when he was eighteen. This was filmed by his Switzerland teammate, Dani Devaud, and found on his old iPhone five. Does this have any relevance to this case?'

Favre looked around at his team and asked the older, red-faced alcoholic-looking detective to begin with his findings.

'Detective Chapuisat, please start first.' At this point Marianne realized she had never asked her older, craggy-looking colleague his name. So, it's *Chapuisat*. A good Vaudois name. We may be related, on my dad's side, she thought to herself.

Chapuisat began. 'Here goes, boss. You asked me to dig into Graff's business activities. His accounts show a lot of transfers to other farmers in the Jorat region. We surmise this is for the carcasses he purchases and freezes, for delivery to the zoo.'

'Any irregularities?' Favre asked.

'Not in the accounts. I was unable so far to find out yet whether meat from cats and dogs had been delivered. For that, I will need to get out there talking to the locals and activate my network.'

'Thanks,' Favre said. 'Keep moving on that. Anything else?'

'Yes, just one thing. Don't know whether it is relevant. Graff sells to a pig farm in the Gros-de-Vaud region.'

Favre was becoming impatient. 'And the relevance?'

149

'This pig farm is high-end, if you could call any pig farm high-end, boss. The pigs are only fed vegetables. No meat products. The farmer sells his meats to delicatessen butchers in expensive neighbourhoods across the country. One of his clients is a deli in Cologny, Geneva, where our man Dirk de Clippele lives.'

'OK. We'll speak to Graff about this.'

Favre asked the younger woman detective to summarize her findings.

'Boss, you asked me to speak to the zoo and to tell them we'd be doing some DNA testing on excrement samples of the boars, lions and tigers. It was a challenge to explain this rationally. I followed your advice and told her about the rumours of meat from domestic pets being in the food supplied to her zoo.'

'How did she react?'

'She was angry. Said she'd call her suppliers immediately to get more details on this.'

'Keep abreast of that, thanks' Favre said.

The older detective piped up again. 'Just one last question, boss. Do you have a theory that glues all this together?'

Favre smiled - a rare occurrence.

'You are right to ask. The short answer is *yes*, but it's complex. Marianne Devaud will explain. She has a *hypothesis* that will take some believing. Over to you, Marianne.'

Marianne's hands started to tremble.

Chapter Forty-Six

The next day, Tuesday, early hours

The night guard at Servion zoo called the fire department at three a.m. He had fallen asleep in a small shed at the bottom end of the park, neat the bison enclosure. He woke up to see smoke and flames at the top end of the zoo, close to where the lions, bears, and tiger enclosures were located. Was it the boar enclosure?

The first firefighters at the scene were the volunteers from the Servion village fire department, including Kevin Gillieron. Kevin was the only one of the volunteer firefighters qualified to use a stun gun should the animals escape. He had brought his gun with him.

The manager of the zoo arrived shortly after Kevin. She met him on the parking side of the entrance, where the volunteers were losing their battle with the flames. She was horrified and worried her animals would be injured. Kevin was more worried that they might escape. Where were the professional firefighters? They should be here by now.

It took the pros over thirty minutes to arrive from the lakeside town of Cully up to the inland village of Servion. Far too long. By the time they arrived, the fire had created an opening in the lion's den, which allowing a lioness to escape. On the other side, some boars had also fled their pen, through the hedge, back into the forest where they had originally been captured a few generations ago. Fortunately, the tiger and bear enclosures had not been touched by the fire, yet.

Within thirty minutes they had the fire under control. The zoo manager checked the enclosures. The boars had bolted, and the lioness had also gone. The male lion had remained and would need to be tranquilized, as he could escape through the same hole the lioness had used. This was quickly done. The young male lion did not even seem to flinch; he was asleep after thirty seconds.

Kevin, in the meantime, had jumped into his old Land Rover and headed off in search of the escaped lioness, armed with his stun gun. He'd seen the animal head over to a farm on the west side of the zoo, where there were cows, horses, and donkeys. He knew the farmer and had called him in advance to warn him. On the phone, the farmer had said he'd get out his military rifle and kill the lioness if he saw her. Kevin pleaded with him not to do this assuring him he would be there within minutes.

Very quickly the firefighters discovered the cause of the fire: arson. The person who had started the fire had left the empty jerrycan of petrol in the boar's pen. The zoo manager confirmed that the jerrycan belonged to the zoo. Inside job? Who would want to put all these animals' lives in danger, never mind having them escape? Animal rights campaigners? Police forensics would arrive later in the day.

By seven in the morning, the story had gone viral. A helicopter hovered above. It was a police helicopter with night and heat vision sensors looking for the escaped lioness. By seven-thirty, the local onlookers had been dispersed and news had gone out on the local radio stations advising anyone within a ten-kilometer distance of Servion to remain indoors. Local schools were ordered to close until further notice.

It wasn't the first time the police helicopters had been called out. The previous year in Epalinges, a suburb north of Lausanne, there had been a sighting of a lioness. A local resident had taken a grainy picture, sent it to the police, and posted it on social media. A massive search operation, with police helicopters involved, followed to hunt the animal down. To no avail. Later the police downgraded their identification of the beast from lioness to large, stray dog. Neither lioness nor dog were spotted again.

Favre remained at the zoo for the rest of the morning, directing operations and waiting for forensics to come up with new *stuff*. In addition to searching for clues, the team was tasked with collecting excrement samples from the boars, tigers, lions, and wolves for analysis.

Ostensibly, as Favre explained to the manager of the zoo, this was to check whether domestic pet meat had been introduced into the supply chain. The real reason was different: they wanted to check for *human* DNA, to verify the validity of Marianne's hypothesis.

Shortly before lunch, the head of the forensics team informed DI Favre they'd found fingerprints on the petrol jerrycan. But they did not match any on the criminal database.

Chapter Forty-Seven

The same day, afternoon, Yves Graff's farmhouse

The zoo manager offered DI Favre lunch at her cafeteria. Favre's copper nose sensed she was a kind, well-intentioned woman acting in the best interests of her animals and her staff. As they tucked into vegetarian moussaka, she was at pains to stress that nobody in her staff team could have possibly set the place alight.

'Detective. Can I ask *why* you want to check the meat I feed my animals? Where did this rumour about cat and dog meat originate Who told you? We are very worried about this issue and would not want it getting into the media.'

'We fully understand that, and you can trust us. This will never get into the media.'

He continued. 'We truly appreciate your help and are not suggesting you've used this meat knowingly. We received some tip-offs from sources in the canton about two unscrupulous veterinary clinics working with the farming community to make some money on the side, with this illegal trade. We'd like to indict them. Any evidence will help, you understand?' Favre was spinning this story. *The end justifies the means.*

Over lunch the zoo manager agreed to accompany DI Favre on his visit to Yves Graff's farm, just five minutes away. Graff had agreed to meet them on condition that the visit didn't last more than forty-five minutes, as he had a fresh meat delivery coming in mid-afternoon.

He'd prepared some coffee and cakes. Not bad for a confirmed, middle-aged bachelor, Favre thought. Out of politeness, they accepted small portions of the black forest gateau served on Graff's late mother's fine bone China.

Favre kicked off the discussion. 'Mr. Graff, you may have heard that the police received disturbing reports of tampering in the meat supply for the zoo.'

Graff knew *most* of his suppliers were straight. But not all. How far should he cooperate? As far as he knew, there was no domestic pet meat in his freezer. What would happen if they found some? Would he be in trouble?

'Detective. How can I put this? I really want to cooperate. It would be easier if I have assurances that I won't be prosecuted if anything compromising is found in my freezers. Remember, I'm just the innocent middleman here.'

'You have my word.'

Favre explained the logistics. His forensics team would take small samples of all the different batches in his freezers. Minimal interference, no damage. Graff agreed.

'Thanks, Mr. Graff. This will be most useful. While I'm here, one additional question. Am I right in assuming that Mr. Dirk de Clippele supplies meat for the zoo?'

'Yes, you are. How did you know?'

'No need for you to worry about that, Mr. Graff. Anything you'd like to tell us about Mr. de Clippele?'

Graff was a stickler for detail, a bit like DI Favre. 'He runs the business from Belgium, not Switzerland. We started purchasing from his family firm last year. He came to me with such amazing prices, I couldn't say no. Almost too good to be true.'

Favre sneered, visibly. 'Indeed. Some things in life *are* too good to be true. How many batches has he delivered?'

'Not enough. I have all the records if you like. There are no more batches from him remaining in my stocks here. They've all been delivered. The last one last week.'

'Thanks. I'd certainly appreciate all the documentation you have regarding this man, including email correspondence.'

'Sure, no problem. I was hoping to get some more supplies from him. I spoke with him yesterday. Unfortunately, his business in Belgium has no surplus at present.'

'Could you tell me more about the conversation you had with him? It could be important for our inquiry.'

Graff was taken aback. 'Is he a suspect?'

'No, not at all. Just a person of interest. As you are. We want to know as much about your suppliers as possible.'

Graff decided to play ball and recounted the full conversation he'd had with de Clippele. Favre asked him to if de Clippele asked *which* animals would be fed with the meat he provided? It was the boars, Graff confirmed.

The boar enclosure at the zoo was where the arsonist had started the fire started in the early hours of the morning, before it spread to other areas. Favre felt he was getting closer. With that thought in his head, his phone vibrated. It was Marianne.

'Boss, it's me. Would you like the good news or the bad news first?'

'Let's go for the good.'

'The lioness has been found and neutralized. In the forest near the Arboretum. She's asleep and being transported back to the zoo now.'

'And the bad news?'

'Kevin Gillieron. He's seriously injured and on his way to the CHUV, the hospital. To intensive care.'

'What happened?'

'He was attacked by the lioness.'

Chapter Forty-Eight

On the same day, evening, The Pastor's residence, Mézières

After the interview with Yves Graff, Philippe Favre did not go back to the office. Instead, he went back home, where he left his PC and police bag and walked next door into the Mézières protestant temple. Véronique, his Pastor wife was waiting for him. Together, they sat in silence. Véronique was praying. Philippe was staring into space.

Today was the anniversary of the tragic death of Philippe's girlfriend in that car accidence when he was just eighteen. Ever since that terrible day, Philippe had battled with guilt and self-doubt. He had become suicidal on several occasions. His wife had tried to teach him how to pray, saying it would help him forgive himself.

He'd tried many things. Psychotherapy. Hypnosis. Long-distance running. None of these had worked. The guilt and the feelings of self-destruction kept returning. In the silence of the church, under the guidance of his wife whom he loved so much, this moment of calm and reflection helped him to be kinder to himself.

Philippe had lost the faith in which he was brought up. The first blow had been the death of his mother, when he was eleven. Then the accident. The police had explained many times to him that it was not his fault. He could not have avoided the collision. For Philippe, this didn't matter. She was gone, like his mother. God, or no God, he'd never see them again, feel their love.

When she'd finished praying, Véronique came over to the pew where Philippe was sitting, sat next to him, and held his hand.

'I'm such a shit,' he said. Véronique said nothing. She held his hand more tightly. Philippe then laid his head on her shoulder. She took him in her arms to comfort him as he broke down in tears.

Chapter Forty-Nine

Two days later, Thursday morning, Blécherette, Police HQ

Favre had called the team meeting for ten that morning, two days after the fire. He knew by then they would have received the results of the DNA testing. In addition to testing the excrement of different meat-eating animals at the zoo, forensics had taken samples of each of the frozen meat batches in the freezers at Yves Graff's farm.

He'd arrived early, as usual. The envelopes containing the results of the analyses were already on his desk. An executive summary had been sent by email. Favre was tempted to open the email first, ridding him of the suspense. True to his disciplined and structured manner, he resisted and opened the first envelope containing the analysis of the batches at Graff's farm. The language was complicated, and the analysis was highly scientific. He skimmed through to the conclusion. Yes, there were traces in three batches of both dog and cat DNA.

He was somewhat surprised. He was also a little annoyed, as this would mean an additional police inquiry, stretching already stretched resources.

For the results from the zoo, instead of opening the second envelope, Favre went straight to the executive summary on his email feed. The summary was more detailed than need be. It also confirmed the presence of cat and dog DNA; but no human DNA had been found in any animal excrement from the boars, the lions, the tigers, and the wolves. No human DNA. Dammit. *Marianne, you messed up, girl. Wrong hypothesis.*

Marianne Devaud did not arrive until past eight-thirty. On her way to her desk, the red-faced older man informed her, discreetly, the boss wanted to see her. Immediately.

Marianne sensed the seriousness in the tone of his voice. She went straight into Favre's office, without knocking. Favre was staring at a thick report. Nobody else was there. Normally he would ask her to sit down. No such niceties this morning, so she remained standing up.

'We've received the results. They are the opposite of what we want, of what your hypothesis predicted. No, your brother and Marco were not fed to the lions, or the boars, or whatever other animal that may enjoy a bit of tasty human. Yes, they found lots of cat and dog DNA, everywhere.'

Marianne was stunned. It made total sense. If the cut-up remains of the bodies of her brother and Marco had not been delivered from Graff's freezer to the zoo, then where had they gone?

'Boss, with respect, are we sure the excrements of the *boars* were analyzed. Unlike the other animals, they eat everything, including the bones.'

'The answer is yes. Very clearly.'

'The boars are still at large, though.'

'Marianne, are you stupid, or what? Our forensics team didn't wait for the boars to shit in front of them while they stood there drinking their coffee. They picked up the excrement from the enclosure that had been left there before the boars bolted.'

Marianne did not like the way her boss was speaking to her. This was unacceptable language. But what could she do? She was an intern and had zero power or influence.

'Boss, leave it to me. I'll get to the bottom of this. Have you cancelled the meeting at ten?'

'Certainly not. We need the help of the rest of the team more than ever. More so, now your hypothesis has been proven to be wrong.'

Marianne left his office, head down. As she was leaving, Chapuisat, the older detective, grabbed her by the arm and almost ordered her to join him for coffee. She followed him to the small staff kitchen. He brought two capsules with him and proceeded to make a short, black expresso for each of them.

He then spoke. 'Look, Marianne, I've been in this place for a long time. I could have retired some years ago, but I would have been restless, and gone back to the bottle. I can see what's happening. He's bullying you, Marianne.'

'Yes, and no. Sometimes I see a little child in him that needs support and encouragement. And then he falls back to his stuck-up, asshole self. Maybe he's a real, shy introvert underneath? Or simply in the wrong job?'

'He's a good detective, Marianne. He's solved some very complex cases. I admire his police skills and his copper's nose. I'd like to help you, so why don't you tell me everything you know about this case, from the beginning. We've got one hour before the team meeting.'

Marianne felt like screaming at full throttle or crying her eyes out. She resisted, and began to tell her story, beginning with the last time Dani Devaud and Marco Zurcher were seen alive at Balthazar's theatre.

Chapulsat listened attentively. Marianne had the impression he was understanding much more than Favre.

At the end of her narrative, he spoke.

'I believe your hypothesis is correct, Marianne. The ambulance used on stage was *not* the one Dirk de Clippele had given to the theatre earlier in the year. It was the *second* one, with four-wheel drive. It was the *replica* he had made in Liège.'

Marianne had also come to the same conclusion. Her older police colleague continued.

'De Clippele, assisted by either Granit Berisha or Anita Patel – maybe both – picked both Dani and Marco up when they collapsed on stage, drugged with scopolamine. They lifted them into the back of the *replica* ambulance when Kevin, unwittingly, cut the electricity. De Clippele had given Kevin different stage instructions requiring him to do this.'

'Makes sense,' Marianne said.

'Marco and Dani's drugged-up bodies were therefore *already* in the back of the *replica* ambulance when Kevin Gillieron drove it off stage and used it later for the solstice.'

'That's it,' Marianne said, relieved.

The older man had not yet finished.

'There is just one deviation, which you could not have predicted in your hypothesis. A few days later, de Clippele transported the human remains to Graff's freezers. He had assumed these remains would be fed to the *boars* at the zoo and consumed entirely, bones included. But they weren't. Yves Graff sold them on to the *high-end* pig farm, without knowing they were human remains. And that's why no human DNA was found in the excrements of the boars at the zoo.'

'Which means the expensive delicatessen pork products sold at specialist delis across the country contain human flesh?'

'Yes…'

Finally, someone was taking Marianne seriously. The older man had one last piece of analysis.

'When Kevin returned to the theatre from his solstice worship with Balthazar and Yves Graff, he parked the *replica* ambulance in the theatre car park. Believing there was still perishables in the back, he hooked the vehicle to the electricity to keep the storage compartment at minus twenty Celsius. When he went home, de Clippele, who was watching, drove the *replica* ambulance with the bodies to the grottos in Mézières, where he camouflaged it with the tarpaulin Paul Porchet had found for him. Anita Patel drove the other mock ambulance back into the parking lot and re-connected the electricity.'

'That's my hypothesis exactly,' Marianne said.

'De Clippele seems to have planned this with meticulous precision, even becoming a *bone fide* meat supplier to Yves Graff to disguise his real intentions.'

Detective Chapuisat was fully aligned with Marianne. And he did not call her *young woman*, unlike the much younger DI Favre.

'What now?' Marianne asked.

'Ideally, we need to get the head of the cantonal police to authorize new DNA testing at the *high-end* pig farm. This case has spent a lot of money on two series of DNA testing. DI Favre must now persuade our head honcho to agree to finance third and final shot.'

'If I ask him to do this, he'll treat me like an idiot. But if you ask?'

'Consider it done, Marianne. That's why I needed to have this coffee with you.'

Marianne was relieved. She had underestimated her older colleague. *Note to self: never judge a person on appearance.*

Three hours later the older detective and Marianne were back in the small cafeteria.

'Surprised?' said the older man. Marianne was ecstatic. 'I didn't think Favre would be so positive. I guess he respects your judgment and your experience.'

'Let's hope our head honcho now plays ball. It's our last chance to find DNA evidence that stands up in court. Without that, no conviction.'

Chapter Fifty

Cologny, Geneva, same day, afternoon

Anita Patel's two teenage children had been allowed a day off school to be with her. At over one-hundred-thousand Swiss Francs per year, per kid, in fees alone, this was an expensive day, Anita thought. They'd better be happy to see me.

The previous evening, they had all dined together in the restaurant of a recently renovated five-star hotel near the school. The new owners were from Shanghai, and their children were at the same boarding school as the Patels; the two families dined together. The four kids finished their meals quickly, left the table and disappeared upstairs to the top-floor suite playing for video games. Anita used the opportunity to sell her legal advisory services in London to her Chinese hosts. Should they ever want to set up a non-domicile status in the UK, she'd be very happy to help. Anita Patel, ever the businesswoman, occasionally the mother.

The following day her kids had decided to remain with their friends and went on a school trip. So much for the planned quality time together.

Anita was drinking a glass of Chardonnay on her large balcony admiring the view of the glistening, snow-covered Alps when her doorbell rang. Police. She opened the door, invited them in, and offered them a glass of wine. They were in no mood for frivolities and immediately told Anita she was being arrested on suspicion of aiding and abetting murder, without specifying who was dead.

The uniformed policeman and woman gave Anita five minutes to prepare a night bag. She went to her bedroom and immediately sent a WhatsApp to Dirk de Clippele. *Big man, I know I'm not supposed to contact you. This message is encrypted, and I'll delete it as soon as it's been sent. You should do this too. You need to know I'm being arrested and taken to Lausanne. You can trust me to remain silent. Love you.*

Dirk de Clippele was sweating hard on an exercise bike in his personal gym in his lakeside mansion. His bodyguard was playing the role of personal trainer that afternoon. Dirk's air pods were connected to his iPhone, which beeped to notify him of Anita's message.

As soon as he read the text, he jumped off the stationary bike and shouted to his bodyguard, 'Activate Plan B.'

The bodyguard immediately ran out of the gym and down the sloping garden lawn to the jetty on the lake. He quickly removed the covering of Dirk's speedboat and started the engines. Back in the house, Dirk put some documents, his phone, and his PC into a small Hermes leather bag and ran down to the jetty. His bodyguard threw him the keys of the speedboat, as their paths crossed, and ran back up to the house just as the Geneva police were arriving at the front door.

Dirk started the engine, pulled back to full throttle, and headed to Yvoire, on the French side of the border, on Lake Geneva.

Back in Villars-Sur-Ollon, Anita had put up no resistance. In the event of her being arrested, Dirk had instructed her to say nothing, to respond to no questions until a well-known Geneva-based criminal lawyer arrived for the interview.

Arriving one hour later at the Vaud Cantonal Police HQ Anita asked to have a quick smoke before being handcuffed and shown to the interview room. Even though she was intent on saying nothing whatsoever, she suspected it would be a long night. She needed her nicotine fix now.

Marianne Devaud was waiting for her in the parking lot. She introduced herself, curtly. No need for formalities and fancy stuff. Anita lit her *Davidoff Slims* and asked Marianne if she cared for one. No. Don't smoke. Never have, never will. Anita was in no hurry to finish her cigarette, sucking the smoke into her lungs as if it would be the last one for a long time. When she'd finished Marianne took the packet of cigarettes from her, as well as her lighter. *Davidoff Slims?* Marianne suddenly had a flashback. The grotto in Mézières. Yes. That's where she found those two cigarette stubs.

Davidoff Slims. Another dot. Another connection.

The twenty-two-kilometre distance from Cologny to Yvoire had taken Dirk less than forty minutes in his two-hundred horsepower speedboat. He docked in the small marina in between two sailboats and stepped ashore, walking the short distance to the nearest restaurant in the old medieval village. The plan was for him to mingle with the tourists until his bodyguard arrived to drive him to his Monaco residence.

Ten minutes later he arrived. Dirk got up to greet him, relieved there was still one person in this world he could trust. They both sat back down. At the table the bodyguard, eyes looking downwards, said just two words - *no choice* - as three French gendarmes entered the restaurant to handcuff and arrest Mr. Dirk de Clippele on suspicion of murder.

Chapter Fifty-One

The next day, nine a.m., interview room, Vaud Canton Police HQ, Blécherette

DI Favre had called an early meeting the following morning for the *Operation Last Seen* team. For the interview sessions, it was vital to get the tactics right. Who interviews whom, and when? Who plays good cop, who plays bad? When to break? And, of course, how to *bluff and use spin* to extract the evidence still needed to have a watertight case that would stand up in court. It needed full alignment and total focus.

Everyone had to play their role. Favre stipulated for all team members, when they weren't in the interview rooms, they must watch proceedings from the observation room.

At six-thirty am all were present, except Marianne Devaud. Just before seven o'clock, Marianne arrived.

'Sorry, everyone, no excuses. Could not sleep.'

Favre, to Marianne's surprise, said he appreciated her honesty. That most others would have faked a bad excuse. Nobody in the room commented.

With Marianne finally there, Favre revealed his plan. They were to play Coach Weymo against Dirk de Clippele, simultaneously. Marianne and Chapuisat would question de Clippele, whilst Favre and the experienced female detective would take on McCauley. They would then break to exchange information and findings.

Coach Weymo was in room one. He was given a duty lawyer, who advised him to remain silent. But Weymo was having none of that. He'd protested and complained non-stop since his arrest at his house in Servion at five a.m. that morning. Having his fingerprints taken was the ultimate insult.

'On what basis have you arrested me, Marianne Devaud? I still don't understand. Aiding and abetting a murder? Who's dead? Look, it's thanks to me that your brother made it big in football. I've nurtured him since he was a little kid, and you were in diapers. I was like a father to you both. You should be helping me get *out* of here, not interviewing me like a common criminal.'

164

The older detective had warned Marianne that Coach Weymo would play the paternalistic, caring football trainer full of milk and honey card. She didn't care.

Marianne showed him Exhibit Number One, the jerrycan from Servion zoo, used to alight the blaze that severely damaged the eastern part of the premises.

'Mr. McCauley, do you recognize this?'

'No. Why would I?'

'Because you found it in a shed in the zoo and used the petrol from this container to start a fire in the boar enclosure at the Servion zoo.'

'That's ridiculous. If you are suggesting I was in any way connected with the fire at the zoo, you are mistaken.'

Marianne knew that forensics would know within thirty minutes whether McCauley's fingerprints were on the handle of the jerrycan. She had time on her side, so she moved on.

'Mr. McCauley. Could you please explain these?' Marianne handed over a file of his bank statements over the past fifteen years. They contained proof of payments from a company registered in Luxembourg.

'I don't need to explain anything. I am allowed to receive money from whoever wants to pay for my services.'

'And what services may they be?'

'That's none of your business.'

'It is the business of the tax authorities, who have informed us they have *no* record of these payments. Oh, and what's more, we have traced the Luxembourg company to a certain Mr. Dirk de Clippele.'

Hearing this Weymo changed tack.

'Sorry, I made a mistake. I always had the intention of declaring this income, seriously.'

'We'll leave you to sort that out with the tax authorities.'

Marianne needed to leave the interview room to receive the results of the fingerprinting on the jerrycan. She handed the questioning over to her older colleague, as planned, and left the room.

The red-faced officer began by asking Coach Weymo if Dirk de Clippele was blackmailing him. Weymo explained they'd worked together for many years. Agent-scout relationship, and that all was transparent, apart from the tax issue. The older detective kept him talking about his dealing with de Clippele, in the hope he'd let something slip, which he didn't.

Five minutes later Marianne returned. There was a match between Weymo's fingerprints and those on the jerrycan. She'd already informed DI Favre about this. Time to squeeze the Scotsman for a confession.

Meanwhile, in interview room number two, DI Favre and the female detective had spent an arduous hour with Dirk de Clippele, who had shown no signs of fatigue, despite having hardly slept. De Clippele's top-notch defence lawyer, the one he'd boasted about to Anita Patel, had called Favre earlier saying he was no longer able to represent de Clippele. *Rats leaving the ship.* Favre had informed de Clippele of this and assigned him a rookie lawyer who was around Marianne's age.

Up to that point, De Clippele had refused to answer any question. Armed with the knowledge that McCauley would admit to starting the fire at the zoo, Favre took a calculated risk.

'Mr. de Clippele. We have proof that you were blackmailing your *scout*, Mr. Ray McCauley. Why?'

De Clippele's face was furious. He was not accustomed to being in a weaker position. 'More like him blackmailing me.'

'And why would he do that?' Favre asked.

De Clippele realized he should have kept his mouth shut. 'No comment.'

Favre had now figured that to get his client to talk, he needed to annoy him, to insult his manhood, to threaten his position of superiority. He continued, with another question.

'Did you pay Mr. Ray McCauley – or Coach Weymo as he's called - to set fire to Servion Zoo?'

De Clippele replied immediately, indignantly, arrogantly.

'No, I didn't. Why would I?'

Favre's mobile vibrated. He took it. It was Marianne. She explained that Ray McCauley had now admitted to receiving twenty-thousand Swiss Francs from Dirk de Clippele to start a fire in the boar enclosure at Servion zoo.

Favre tried to hide the smile wanting to burst out of his face. They were winning.

'Mr. de Clippele. Did you pay Mr. Ray McCauley twenty-thousand francs to start a fire in the boar enclosure at Servion zoo.'

'And why would I want to do that?'

'Because you knew we'd find human DNA, probably in the excrement of the boars. Because they were fed the cut-up bodies of Dani Devaud and Marco Zurcher, who you drugged and kidnapped from Balthazar's theatre with the assistance of Mrs. Anita Patel.'

'Don't bring *Pattie* into this. She is innocent.'

Favre smiled to himself again. It's working. *Make it personal.*

He continued. 'I'm talking about Mrs. Anita Patel, your lawyer, and your lover. The woman who is also in custody here and being interviewed as we speak. The woman who smokes *Davidoff Slims*. Funny. We found cigarette butts of the same brand in the grottos in Mézières. Is that where you hid the bodies, in the *replica* ambulance?'

'No comment.'

A uniformed officer entered the room with Ray McCauley's confession.

'Thank you, officer. Mr. de Clippele. Allow me to read aloud the declaration that we have just received from Mr. Ray McCauley.

I, Mr. Ray McCauley, hereby confirm the following:

1. *I entered Servion zoo late afternoon on the date in question.*
2. *One of my former players at FC Jorat Mézières works at the zoo. He showed me the shed where he keeps his tool, including a jerrycan of petrol, and I stole the keys to the shed from him.*
3. *I then was able to hide, undetected, in the toilets in the cafeteria until after midnight.*
4. *I set fire to the boar enclosure at around two-thirty a.m. I did this by using the petrol that I found in the above-mentioned work shed.*
5. *I deeply regret my actions. I was specifically instructed by Mr. Dirk de Clippele to destroy the boar enclosure. Unfortunately, the fire got out of hand and spread to other spaces.*
6. *I was paid twenty-thousand francs to do this by Mr. Dirk de Clippele.*
7. *I have no idea why Mr. Dirk de Clippele wanted me to set fire to the boar enclosure.*

Signed and dated, Raymond S. McCauley'

While Favre read this, Dirk de Clippele did not flinch. He did not even blush. His eyes barely moved; he hardly blinked, like a block of steel.

Favre knew he now had enough evidence to charge de Clippele with hiring Coach Weymo set fire to the zoo. But not enough to charge him with the murder of Dani Devaud and Marco Zurcher.

For it to be watertight in a court of law, all they now needed were DNA traces of Dani and Marco from the *high-end* pig farm. With that, Favre was certain they'd be home and dry. His boss just had to sign the order.

They took a break.

Chapter Fifty-Two

Twenty minutes later, interview room number one, Police HQ, Blécherette

DI Favre had interviewed many people over his career. Dirk de Clippele was somewhere between *narcissistic superiority* and *sociopathic cool*. The only way to break his shield was to for after his ego and to get personal. He'd succeeded a couple of times that morning, but the psychological effort was draining his energy.

For the next interview session, he decided to replace the younger female detective with Chapuisat, believing he would give him more psychological support.

The two men were about to enter the interview room for the second session when Marianne arrived, in a flush.

'Boss, it's not good. *Head honcho* refused to authorize the pig farm DNA testing. Said it would stretch the budget too far; that the past two times were inconclusive, so why would this be any different? I tried to persuade him, but it's no. Sorry, boss.'

Favre didn't say anything. Chapuisat whispered something in his ear, and the two of them spent the next few minutes back in Favre's office discussing tactics.

Twenty minutes later they were back in the interview room with Dirk de Clippele. Chapuisat took the lead after DI Favre had started the audio recording.

'Mr. de Clippele. We have just received the DNA results from the zoo. We analyzed the excrement of the boars and we found traces of human DNA. Traces of the DNA of Mr. Daniel Devaud and Mr. Marco Zurcher, clients of yours, I believe.'

De Clippele remained poker-faced. Chapuisat continued.

'We can prove you paid Mr. Ray McCauley to set fire to the boar enclosure at the zoo. We believe you did this to prevent the police from finding DNA evidence of the two missing footballers in the boar excrement.'

De Clippele still didn't flinch.

'We also tested the batches of the meat you sold to Yves Graff. There was a batch remaining that had not yet been delivered to the zoo. This also contained DNA traces of the two said clients of yours. In addition, we found tyre track marks of the same *replica* ambulance you had reworked in Liège. We found these at the grottos in Mézières, where Anita Patel dropped a couple of stubs of her *Davidoff Slims* cigarettes. Shall I continue, Mr. de Clippele?'

Favre was impressed. How could his older colleague *spin* all this without blinking? And then he remembered. Chapuisat was a reformed alcoholic. He'd been bluffing and spinning most of his adult life, mainly to himself.

Dirk de Clippele did not say a word. His rookie lawyer seemed totally oblivious to the proceedings.

Chapuisat continued.

'As a result of such overwhelming evidence, Mr. de Clippele, and there is more, we will be charging you and Mrs. Anita Patel with the *murder* of Messrs. Daniel Devaud and Marco Zurcher. Do you have anything to say?'

The word *murder* hit home, as did the accusation against his lover, Anita Patel, *Pattie*, the only woman he'd ever managed to love. The only woman who'd fully grasped his primordial, instinctive need for control, for power, for money. Why had he been such a shit to her the other day?

The *big man* took a few minutes to think. For the first time, his head slumped, his hands clasped his cheekbones, eyes down. *Pattie* must be saved. She'd wait for him, surely. He knew that because she loved him. He'd go down for her. At that precise moment, Dirk figured he would not be making love with Anita Patel for a long time.

He lifted his head, smiled, and began to explain, point-by-point how he, and *he alone*, had killed Dani Devaud and Marco Zurcher.

He'd added scopolamine – the *date rape* drug - to their drinks at the table. Dressed up as Santas with white beards, they were drinking their orange juices through straws. It was easy to spike them. He'd timed it so they would collapse on the stage at the entr'acte.

He'd written out different stage instructions for Kevin Gillieron, requiring him to cut the electricity for the whole building when the two Santas fell on the floor. In the dark and the panic, he'd lifted the drugged bodies of the two footballers into the ambulance on the stage. Before the show, he'd replaced the mock ambulance with the *replica* he'd commissioned in Liège, with a four-wheel-drive to allow him to drive the bodies into the woods and hide the vehicle in the grotto in Mézières later that night.

Favre then asked him what he knew about Kevin, Yves, and Balthazar using the ambulance? De Clippele replied that it was *not* part of his plan. Kevin was supposed to just drive the ambulance offstage and onto the parking lot at the back of the theatre. De Clippele explained that this had flummoxed him for a while. Fortunately, after their solstice worship, Kevin returned the vehicle to the parking area. By this time the occupants were probably already dead. De Clippele then finished his account of the evening by saying that Anita Patel had *nothing* to do with this whatsoever.

As Dirk was telling his version of the murder, Chapuisat was making notes. When he'd finished, he asked Dirk to stand up. The wily old detective then lay, face down on the floor, and asked Dirk to lift him onto the small coffee table in the corner of the interview room. Impossible. Dirk tried three times but was unable to lift the older detective onto the coffee table.

Chapuisat then explained, calmy, that he was about the same weight as Marco Zurcher, the taller and heavier of the two footballers Dirk claimed to have lifted into the ambulance on stage, with no assistance from anyone else.

'Seems like you've lost a lot of strength over the past three months, Mr. de Clippele? Very strange.'

The wily old detective smiled, tobacco-stained teeth on full show.

'Are you sure you lifted those bodies alone into the vehicle, Mr. de Clippele? If Mrs. Anita Patel didn't help you, could it have been Mr. Granit Berisha?'

Dirk de Clippele replied he had no further comment.

DI Favre terminated the interview just after three o'clock in the afternoon. He was shattered. De Clippele was draining him of all his energy quicker than any other suspect he'd interviewed so far in his professional career.

171

Chapter Fifty-Three

Same day, interview room number one, afternoon session

Marianne Devaud and the female detective were briefed by DI Favre before they began their first interview with Anita Patel. They were given copies of Dirk de Clippele's signed declaration, in which he confessed to kidnapping and murdering Dani and Marco, *alone*. Alone?

Anita Patel had been assigned the same rookie. She immediately spoke out.

'I am not accepting this lawyer. Is he even qualified? Can you get him his milk bottle, please? Looks like the baby's hungry.'

The female detective replied on the bounce. 'And which lawyer would you like to have?'

'The same one as Mr. Dirk de Clippele.'

Marianne pounced. 'Is Mr. de Clippele on the premises? Do you know his lawyer?'

Anita backed off.

'I don't know whether he is here or not. I was told I was arrested concerning the disappearance of two football players who were clients of his, so I assumed he was here.'

The female detective continued. 'Let's begin, shall we? Mrs. Patel. Can you confirm that you smoke *Davidoff Slims* cigarettes?'

'Yes, why?'

'Can you confirm you accompanied Mr. Dirk de Clippele on the night of the fundraising event for FC Jorat Mézières at Balthazar's Theatre in Servion, Switzerland?'

'Yes.'

'Were you also disguised as a Santa, along with Messrs. De Clippele, Berisha, Devaud, and Zurcher?'

'That's correct, yes.'

'Was it difficult for you and Dirk de Clippele to pick up Marco Zurcher and Dani Devaud, when they collapsed on the floor?'

'*Yes, it was.* It was pitch dark. Dirk asked me to help get them into the vehicle on the stage, which, he told me, would take them immediately to hospital.'

The two women interviewing Anita Patel tried to hide their surprise at her reply. Marianne whispered something into the other woman's ear, and they both left the interview room for around five minutes. While they were away, Anita pleaded with the guard in the room to allow her out for a smoke. He refused.

Back in the interview room, the questioning continued. Marianne went first.

'Mr. de Clippele has now admitted to the murder of Dani Devaud and Marco Zurcher.'

'Impossible. I was with him the whole evening. Dirk would not do anything like that. Believe me. He's a good man. A bit shy. That's why he needs me.'

Marianne jumped in again. 'And why did he need you in the grotto in Mézières in that same ambulance. We know you were there because we have your DNA on two cigarette stubs you left there. Helping him cut up the bodies, Mrs. Patel, for delivery to the animals at the zoo?'

'Don't be ridiculous, young woman.'

'Mrs. Patel, unless you come up with a better explanation, we will arrest you for aiding and abetting the murder of Messrs. Daniel Devaud and Marco Zurcher. Have you anything else to say?'

'You can't do that. I'm innocent.'

'Explain to us *how* you are innocent, Anita. Or shall I call you *Pattie*?' Marianne was feeling vindictive. She did not like being called a young woman, even though she was. Time to force the issue.

Anita took some time to think, and then started talking.

'OK, I'll tell you. After the theatre chaos I needed a drink. We went to a restaurant in Essertes, La Croix-Fédérale, I think. We stayed there until closing, past midnight. Dirk then drove around the woods. He said he wanted to find somewhere to make out. Which was strange because he didn't seem to be in the mood.

Eventually we arrived at a sort of a grotto, I don't know where. We stayed there a while. I had a couple of cigarettes. He then told me to drive his car away from the grotto and to wait somewhere else in the woods until he called me. It was cold and I was fed. I found a place in another wood and fell asleep. Good job I had my fur coat to keep me warm. I was woken up around three a.m. when Dirk called, instructing me to pick him up at Balthazar's theatre. It was all very strange.'

Marianne and her colleague exchanged glances. This was not what they expected to hear. They needed to consult again. A second break. This time the guard was instructed to take Anita for a smoke break in the designated area. He gave her back her packet of *Davidoff Slims*.

Chapter Fifty-Four

Designated smoking-room, Police HQ, Blécherette

Marianne and her colleague were still in discussion when the duty guard who had escorted Patel to the smoking room called. He explained that Mrs. Patel had something *very important* to say, but would only speak with Marianne Devaud, and no one else. And only in the smoking-room. Marianne went down to the smoking-room. She hated cigarette smoke, but figured it was part of the job to be taken out of one's comfort zone occasionally.

Anita Patel was unaware of the hidden video camera connected to the central observation room, where the female detective would follow the discussion between Marianne and Anita.

The smoking room had no seats, so Marianne brought two big cushions into the smoking-room and invited Anita to join her, sitting together on the floor, yoga-style. *Surreal.*

'What is it you'd like to say to me in private, Mrs. Patel?' Marianne was now playing good cop, nice cop, almost sisterly.

Anita lit a cigarette and began her story.

'I know who you are, Marianne. I knew your brother well, Dani Devaud.'

Marianne was immediately shocked by her use of the *past tense*.

'Dirk and I *created* his football career. We nurtured him. I made sure he had the best legal contracts. He did well at Everton FC, but they had higher ambitions and let him go. At Wigan Athletic FC he was adored by the fans and is still missed as we speak.'

Marianne interrupted. 'Where are you going with this?'

Anita continued. 'Problem was, Dani knew *too much*, didn't he? About one person. You know who I'm talking about. Granit Berisha. The man who will probably become the best Liverpool FC player in the club's history. If he is given the time. He needs another five years. We don't want any scandals that would taint his reputation with the fans, do we? Liverpool supporters adore him. Ha. If only they knew he was gay.'

Marianne was beginning to get it. Anita was aware of the video that her brother made of Granit in Sitges. She interrupted again.

'Who else knows about that video, Mrs. Patel?'

'I do. Dirk knows. Granit knows, and so does Emina, his wife. Personally, I didn't think it was a big deal. If your brother had wanted to blackmail Granit, why now? Makes no sense. He'd have done it years ago.'

Marianne agreed.

'That's right. I think he'd completely forgotten about it.'

She was on the verge of adding she'd discovered the video on an old iPhone at her mum's place. Instead, she desisted and reminded herself not to get too *comfortable* with Anita.

'Tell me more about Emina, Granit's wife, Mrs. Patel.'

A smile came to Anita's face.

'She is adorable. I discovered her; you know? Me. It was *my* idea to hook her up with Granit. Suited both of them, didn't it? Luigi, her man in Milan, the father of her daughter, is married and will never leave his wealthy wife. Emina was going to make a scandal of it when she fell pregnant, go to the press, blackmail him. Luckily, I got there first and thought up this arrangement.'

'What arrangement, Mrs. Patel?'

'Simple. I set up a white wedding between Emina and Granit. I wrote the contract which guaranteed her twenty percent of Granit's total earnings. And it's a done deal.'

'And what did *you* get out of this?'

'Information, young woman. Knowledge is power. You'll learn, one day. Emina sent me copies of *all* Granit's texts with Dirk de Clippele, without them ever knowing.'

'How did you do this?'

'Emina knew Granit's phone password. Every night when he was asleep, she took screenshots of the *WhatsApp* messages with Dirk and sent them to me.'

'Did you keep them?'

Marianne realized that was a stupid question.

'Yes. As a bargaining chip. Just in case I got arrested. And here we are. I'm certain they'd stand up in court. They are explosive. So why don't you run off and tell your little boss that I'm waiting for him? Here. And tell him to bring me a new pack of cigarettes. *Davidoff Slims.*'

Chapter Fifty-Five

On the same day, evening, interview room number one

One hour later, Favre arrived at the smoking room. He introduced himself politely to Anita. They had never met. Being a secret smoker, Favre was happy to have a sneaky cigarette every now and then, even if it was a *Davidoff Slims*, a ladies' brand.

Anita cooperated fully. Favre told her the judge would certainly look more favourably on her sentence if she gave them all the *WhatsApp* messages she'd kept. Anita opened her phone, there and then, and airdropped over three hundred texts between Dirk and Granit directly to Favre's mobile phone. He sent them to Marianne.

It did not take Marianne long to find the thread of messages which inculpated both Dirk de Clippele and Granit Berisha in the murder of Dani and Marco. And they were explosive.

Dirk de Clippele was led back into the same interview room in which he'd been questioned that morning. The one used to question Anita Patel in the afternoon. As he entered, he knew that *Pattie* had been in that same room. He smelled her presence. Anita always wore the same perfume, a very rare and expensive brand.

She's been here? In this room? They are playing us against each other, he thought. He was certain his *Pattie* would have been strong and upright. She would certainly not have said anything to compromise him.

'Good evening, Mr. de Clippele,' Favre began.

'I would like to thank you for being so candid earlier and for your declaration in which you state you were solely responsible for the kidnapping and murder of those two young footballers. Yes, you were candid. And yes, you are still hiding some very important elements.'

Dirk replied with a disdainful *no comment*.

DI Favre continued. 'I'm going to ask my colleague, Marianne Devaud, to read aloud some of the *WhatsApp* messages Mrs. Patel gave us earlier today.'

'Yes, Detective Inspector. I'll begin with this one. Granit Berisha to Dirk de Clippele. *Dirk, you have a choice. Eliminate them, or no contract renewal.*

Don't forget, the latest offer from the video-gaming company for my exclusive use of my avatar is now worth more than ten million.'

'What do have to say about that, Mr. de Clippele?' Favre asked.

Dirk remained silent. Marianne continued.

'Another message. This time from Dirk to Granit. *I can't do it alone. I'm going to need your help. Anita cannot know that I'm going to kill them. OK with you Granit?*'

Again, no comment from Dirk.

Favre was enjoying this.

'I wonder why Granit didn't reply. I guess he wants *you* to shoulder all the blame. Pretty useless now. He's being arrested as we speak in Liverpool by our colleagues at Merseyside Police. Any comments, Mr. de Clippele?'

Once again, Dirk remained silent.

'Mr. de Clippele, we have over three hundred texts between you and Mr. Granit Berisha. We have more than enough to lock you and him away for a long time. Mrs. Patel will get a lighter sentence, as she cooperated with us, as will Mr. Ray McCauley. We understand why you wanted to protect your lover, Anita Patel. But why do you want to protect Granit Berisha? We just don't get it?'

Finally, Dirk spoke. 'I'm a businessman, Detective Inspector Favre. You know that. What difference would it make to my verdict if Granit is sentenced or not?'

Favre agreed it would not make any difference. Just one more prisoner for the Swiss taxpayer.

'Exactly,' Dirk commented. 'So why would I have wanted Berisha in prison, when he could make me lots more money playing football and selling his avatar to rich videogame companies. I have a copy of that video Dani filmed in Sitges in a place nobody will ever know. I could continue to blackmail him until I got out of prison fifteen years on good behaviour. Guess I didn't plan on Mrs. Patel betraying me, did I?'

Chapter Fifty-Six

Next day, morning, Operations Room, Police HQ, Blécherette

Favre had scheduled the team meeting's briefing for ten that morning. He began by explaining that Marianne Devaud was taking some time off. How she'd managed to control her emotions over the past few months in an admirable display of stoicism and self-control. How de Clippele's confession last night had proven her hypothesis. A hypothesis Favre had believed from the start.

At this point, Chapuisat coughed, as if clearing his throat.

Favre went on to explain how Marianne had broken down completely the previous evening and would now be spending some weeks in consultation with a therapist. Favre wasn't sure if she'd ever complete her Ph.D. or return to her internship at HQ. He thanked her for all her work, without which they'd have never solved the case.

As for Granit Berisha, he'd been arrested in Liverpool and would be flown to Switzerland where he would await trial along with Dirk de Clippele and Anita Patel. The police expect twenty-five years for De Clippele and Berisha and ten years for Patel.

Emina Berisha, Favre explained, had already filed for divorce and moved with her daughter to Milan.

Yves Graff continues to deny any wrongdoing. A retired teacher living opposite told us he'd seen the mock ambulance parked at Graff's farm just after the new year. They could not identify the driver, though we think it was de Clippele. We are not pressing charges against Graff. However, several Swiss delicatessen shops are taking him to court for abuse of trust.

DI Favre concluded the meeting by thanking all the team for their excellent work and inviting them all to the upcoming show at Balthazar's Theatre, a musical based on the life of Al Capone.

Chapter Fifty-Seven

Three months later, Balthazar's Theatre

Marianne Devaud followed a total of ten sessions with her therapist She and Kenosha decided to move in together in Mollie-Margot, not far from her home village, Mézières. The murder inquiry had brought them much closer, and they were both now committed to settling down together.

She loved the city of Lausanne but realized her mother needed her nearby, and she needed her mother close as well, to share their mutual grief. Paul Porchet had now moved in permanently with her mother. Those two also made a good match. Kenosha had persuaded her to continue her internship and Ph.D., and she'd planned to return to DI Favre's team by September.

Before then there was one thing she needed to do for full closure.

It was seven in the evening, and she knew her host would be in his office. A new show was having its première at his theatre. She decided *not* to call Kevin Gillieron in advance, fearing he'd not want to see her.

Arriving at the theatre, Marianne knocked gingerly on Kevin's office door. No reply. She entered to find it empty. As she was peering inquisitively into the drink's cabinet, Kevin returned, still limping slightly from his injuries.

'Marianne Devaud. Nice to see you. But only if you're *not* here on police business. I heard that both Dirk de Clippele and Granit Berisha got the maximum of twenty-five years. Surprised that Anita Patel got off with just five. Weren't you?'

'Kevin, I don't want to talk about that. I'm here on another subject.'

Kevin appeared a changed man. Confident, head and shoulders upright, and looking at Marianne straight in the eyes, kindly, with no aggression.

'I'm listening. But first, can I ask you to pour me a glass of *Aberlour* from the cabinet. My arm is still giving me trouble. Hope that lioness enjoyed her small chunk of Gillieron flesh. She got me from behind. Too quick for me to use my stun gun. Lucky to be alive, I suppose.'

'Sorry to hear that, Kevin. I read the articles in the *24 Heures*. You were the hero of the moment. And you deserve all the praise. Incredible.'

'What was it you wanted to tell me?'

'We eventually got the results of the DNA back from the bodies we dug up at the menhir site.'

'And…'

'Well, how can I put this?'

'Whichever way you put it, Marianne, don't worry. I'm beyond that. I told Yves I'm finished with all this solstice stuff, and if my dad was the result of incest, so be it. I'm ok with it.'

'He wasn't, Kevin. The DNA showed no connection with yours'

Kevin looked relieved. 'So, how did they die?'

'We don't know. No sign of injuries, poison, or suicide. I guess it will remain a mystery.'

'That's the problem with small village life, you see Marianne. Mysteries turn into suppositions, which turn into accusations which then become fact. Like my dad being the son of siblings.'

'I'm sorry you had to go through all of that. Was your father's name David?'

'Yes, why do you ask?'

Marianne opened her shoulder back and took out an old black, hardback, A4-sized bound document and handed it over to Kevin.

'What's this?'

'I believe it's your father's thesis for his bachelor's degree in History at Lausanne University.'

Kevin looked opened it and read the title out loud.

'The Servion Solstice Sect: A Two-Thousand-Year-Old Tradition? Author, David Gillieron. Well, yes, I guess that's my father?'

'It's for you, Kevin. I'm going to leave you in peace to read this alone. Just one observation before I leave. It appears that the rumour of your father began after he submitted his thesis to Lausanne University. In my humble opinion, in all the interviews he did with families in Servion and the wider Jorat region, he must have stumbled upon some information that someone wanted to keep secret. That someone decided to start the erroneous and pernicious rumour that your dad was the product of incest. You have all my sympathy, Kevin. *Adieu.*'

With these words Marianne walked out of Kevin's office, without looking back.

Kevin watched her go, then opened the two-hundred-page hardbound document. He began by reading the *academic abstract* at the beginning of the thesis.

The village of Servion in Vaud Canton is located on the road to the Roman city of Avenches, a settlement created in the first century, then named Aventicum.

At the time of the Roman empire, the surrounding region was inhabited by Helvetians, a Celtic tribe, which strived to retain its customs and traditions, often against the wishes of their Roman rulers.

When the Romans invaded their territory, the Helvetians made solidarity pacts between family groupings in the Jorat region, where Servion now stands. The goal was to maintain their culture in the face of Roman opposition.

The Helvetian Celts never fully accepted the Roman lifestyle, with the Helvetian women remaining strong and independent, in contrast to the inferior roles' women held in Roman society.

The five-thousand-year-old menhir standing near the village of Servion was a place of worship for the Helvetian Celts habiting the Jorat region. The whole community came together four times a year for the Solstice and Equinox celebrations.

Each region had its own high druid and high druidess. The specific tradition in Servion was that the druid and druidess were always brother and sister. However, the druid and druidess roles were not hereditary. Each generation of elders, both male and female, nominated the future high druid and high druidess when they were just twenty-one years old. Always brother and sister.

As soon a druid or druidesses died, the new sibling couple began their duties and held their roles for life. Although the druid and druidess were considered 'divine', they were not allowed to be part of the group of community elders and had no political or decision-making power.

The only official task they had to perform was to manage the celebrations of the Solstice and Equinox, four times per year at the site of the menhir.

These celebrations created and cemented strong bonds between families in their struggles to resist Roman rule. This worship was kept secret from the Roman authorities and nobody, other than people of Celtic descent, was allowed to take part.

Over the centuries the worshippers integrated Christianity into their Solstice and Equinox routines, always beginning their nights of worship at the chapel, and terminating at the menhir, passing the cemetery along the way. In this way they believed they would maintain an unbreakable connection and presence with their deceased ancestors.

Like other Celtic tribes, Helvetians followed an oral tradition, passing down stories and legends from generation to generation by word of mouth, which means we have no written records of these.

According to such stories passed orally from generation to generation, it is said that in the Middle Ages the brother-and-sister high druid and druidess from the ruling 'de Sarvyon' family decided they were not just 'divine', they were also permitted to produce their own offspring, for the 'benefit' of the local community.

From the information passed down orally until the present day, it appears this decision was never revoked.

This Lausanne University Department of History Bachelor's degree thesis aims to shed some light on the activities of the Servion Solstice Sect today by examining and analysing its activities over the past two-thousand years.

The information and data for this work were gathered from personal interviews carried out with forty-two residents of Servion and the surrounding Jorat region. Names have been changed to preserve their identities.

David Gillieron

Epilogue

An op-Ed piece by Sanjay Singh, Editor-in-chief, Liverpool Post

Last week one of Liverpool FC's greatest ever players, along with his agent, were jailed in Switzerland for a minimum of twenty-five years for the murder of two other footballers.

You all know why they were sent down, and rightly so. But why did they do it? Sadly, this tragic case asks more questions than it answers.

How many gay male footballers play in the English Premier League? And why is it so hard for them to come out.? To live their natural lives, to be in tune with their feelings, their emotions, and their loved ones, without fearing a backlash from the sport in which they excel.

I'm not saying we need to be constantly informed about the sexual orientation of our favourite players. I'm just saying it should *not be an issue*!

I'm simply stating it should be *easy and natural* for them to come out if they so wish.

But it isn't. You know that. I know that.

The English Premier League has twenty teams, with an average of twenty-five professional players employed by each. Some of the richer teams have more. Let's say five hundred players in total. If ten percent are gay, reflecting the same proportion in the national population, that makes fifty gay football players in the EPL.

Where are they? Who are they? Why is it, when so many sports are now opening, up football, or *soccer* as it's called in some countries, remains so locked down and closed to gay players coming out?

Questions that need answers, readers, if we want to avoid such unnecessary tragedies in the future.

Acknowledgements

Many thanks to Andy E and Andy G, to Brenda, Andrea, Ingrid, Matt, Stephanie, Stevie, and Vincent for reading the Beta Version of this novel and giving me invaluable feedback. I salute you all, and I owe you one, maybe two!

Many thanks to such a great group of friends and acquaintances in the village of Servion and from the whole Jorat region. I hope you'll still want to be friends with me once you've finished reading this novel 😊

Printed in Great Britain
by Amazon